TELL ME WHAT I WANT TO HEAR

a novel by
Stephen F. Davitt

TELL ME WHAT I WANT TO HEAR

Editor-in-chief: Clarinda Harriss
Editor and Executive Proofreader: Leah Bushman
Editor: Maddie Yoest
Graphic Design: Ace Kieffer
Front Cover Photo: Michael Fevang
Front Cover Model: Alex Hewett
Back Cover Photo: LIFE AMONG THE TULIPS Magazine

Beignet Books
a subsidiary of BhB, Inc.

Baltimore, Maryland
"Baltimore needs beignets"

Distributor: Itasca Books, Inc.

ISBN: 978-1-938144-80-6

Printed in the United States of America

For Lilly and Emilie, le moghrá go léir

Table of Contents

Death in the Park

1: October 21, 1919, Morning after the crime: Baltimore

A raw wind blows in off the harbor and kicks the ground fog off like a blanket. The cold damp air finds its way through a labyrinth of narrow cobblestone streets. Around the feet of General Robert E. Lee's bronze statue, the fog swirls like the devil's breath. On his pedestal, the General stands guard over the city park with complete disinterest. The grass is a faded green, the trees are orange and brown. Police officers, blue. There was a murder here last night.

The victim is laid out with his arms outstretched and his pants down around his ankles. Blood spills from two wounds to the abdomen. There is an ice pick still poking out from his throat.

A plainclothes detective looks around the crime scene. Frost covers everything except the body. He grunts as he squats down to make closer observations. The cold weather makes his limbs ache. The blood is still wet and congealing from fresh wounds, yet the victim's shoes, pants cuffs, and white apron are smeared with dried blood.

A camera shutter falls like a guillotine. The detective looks up and sees a Baltimore Herald photographer documenting the scene. A scrawny character in an ill-fitting herringbone suit moves around the victim.

"Do you really need to do that?" The detective asks. This guy looks more like a vaudeville character than a news photographer. "His kin don't know yet."

"I bet the missus or the mother will be proud to hear how he passed on." The photographer takes another photograph. "What do you think happened?"

The detective gets up with another grunt and pushes the news photographer back. Men from the morgue move in and perform their task.

"Be careful with the ice pick. Looks like some good fingerprints on it," the detective reminds the men. "I've already found a barber's razor in the grass. It may have prints on it as well. This might be the only evidence we get."

"Don't worry, sir," one of the men replies. "We'll take good care of things. We're going to leave it in till we get to the morgue. That's the coroner's job, sir."

"Excellent." The detective nods.

"Come on, give me something," says the photographer, "I'll hold the pictures till you tell his folks, but you have to give me something to start with." He lights up a cigarette and flips the matchstick away. "Gimme a break. What's with the arms stretched out like he's some kind of Jesus with his pants down? Looks a bit insane. Isn't there a Saint Suffering Somebody Church nearby?"

"Listen, I don't have much, so I don't need rumors getting started." The detective weighs his options and decides to control the story. "What do you want to know?"

"Thanks. First, what's your name? So I can quote you." The photographer is one of those guys who can keep a lit cigarette on his lip while he talks.

"Majewski. Detective Stanley Majewski. Southern District."

"Thanks. Eichenberg, Freddy Eichenberg. Baltimore Herald." Juggling his camera gear, he nods while taking notes. "So what happened?"

"This is still only a guess. From the looks of the victim, he may have worked down in Pigtown. We'll be looking to see who hasn't turned up for work. From there we hope to track down his family." Majewski wants to walk away, but the newsman keeps stepping in his path.

"It appears he came here looking for…" Majewski points to the secluded part of the park near the statue of General Lee. "This area is known for ladies of the night offering their services."

"You mean he was looking for a whore."

"I think he was expecting to be serviced when he was attacked and robbed. From the smell on him, I'm guessing whoever it was took advantage of his inebriated state. He hasn't a penny on him." Majewski stands by his explanation and wants to go about his business.

"Look at the size of this bastard. This guy must have had quite a load on for someone to take him down like this." Eichenberg writes in his notebook that the victim stood over six feet, had the enormous arms of a laborer, blond hair, must have been in his late twenties, maybe early thirties.

"What about the pose? Why did he get it in the stomach and throat? Seems a bit excessive, don't you think?" Eichenberg is interested in the horrible details. "Those wounds, they look like, what are they called… *stig, stag* something. What's it called?"

"Stigmata." Majewski shakes his head. He was a well-schooled Catholic lad. "Stigmata wounds are on the hands, feet, and side of the ribs. This fellow's wounds are in the stomach, under the ribs, and you see the ice pick in the throat. So I'd say no."

"Gimme a break, I didn't go to one of those mackerel-snapping schools. What do I know? Still—the crazy death pose. Do you think some religious zealot went overboard?" Eichenberg prays for a sensational hook for a byline.

"I haven't ruled anything out." Majewski turns his back and walks away with a slight limp. Was it a pose or coincidence, the way the arms splayed out? A religious act of vengeance on the wicked or a simple robbery? That leaves a lot of motive in between. Indeed, dignity was no longer an issue to the victim. Majewski makes a deal with himself and God: to die with his pants on.

2: October 21, 1919, 8:30 am: Pigtown, Baltimore

Majewski makes his way through the narrow streets of Pigtown. Buskers and A-rabbers—their decorated horse drawn carts filled with the year's last watermelons—compete with motorcars, trucks, and trollies for dominance on Washington Street. Neighborhood kids dart through the traffic with immortal daring. Cattle and hogs march toward their destinies for the benefit of the citizenry. The stench of animal piss and shit masks the stench of human piss and shit. This is the glory of Pigtown. The past and future collide here. The Great War is over. American destiny is limitless. Electricity, telephones, motorcars, and new ideas are slick and clean, but Pigtown still relies on the messy business of old-time slaughter and manpower.

Majewski draws a deep breath as he absorbs the number of possible places a butcher might work. Slaughterhouses and butcher shops line the streets. Advertisements for Esskay Meats—S. K, for good German names Schluderberg and Kurdle—hang like artwork in an open-air museum. Signs for kosher, German, Italian, and Polish specialty meats flap on anything that isn't a window or door. All around him he sees the underclass hard at work. Thumb-bearing ants maneuver carts loaded with meats and merchandise, bound for neighborhoods with lawns and gardens.

The investigation begins with the first shop he sees. The inquiry questions are all the same: Has an employee failed to show up for work today? If so, what did he look like? Was he religious? Did he drink? Did he have friends or enemies? The questioning goes on throughout the morning and into the afternoon.

Majewski's hips feel as if they're being crushed by a mortar and pestle. The pain is a counterweight to any optimism he has for a lead. A full day of pounding the pavement takes its toll. He makes a deal with his aching joints: one more stop. The detective enters the American Meat Company just before the office closes.

"Excuse me—Detective Majewski, Baltimore Police Department. Do you mind if I ask you a few questions?" Majewski displays his badge and makes his way into a cramped office. The clerk's nameplate sits prominently on his desk: "Mr. Schlamp. Office Manager."

A round, balding man, his glasses sliding down his nose, looks up from his ledgers. He answers with a blank stare and head nod.

"Has anyone not reported for work today?" Majewski asks without the same hope he had in the morning.

"Our shifts start at 6 am sharp." The office clerk searches through some papers without looking up. "I see we were down one man today."

"Do you have a name?" Majewski's eyes light up, but he keeps hope in his hip pocket.

Still not looking up, the clerk scrutinizes another pile of papers. "I see we are missing a Mr. Henry Weiss."

"Can you describe Mr. Weiss and tell me his occupation?" Majewski has his notebook ready.

After looking at another pile of papers and some shuffling around, the clerk offers his attention and removes his glasses.

"Mr. Weiss is a congenial employee, works the line in dispatching the livestock. He has been working here since he returned from France and the war. He is a large man, over six foot. Blond hair, grey eyes. Very muscular. Well suited for this type of work."

"That is very helpful. Thank you." Majewski's head is down as he scribbles notes. "Did he have any problems with anyone here? Was he prone to drinking?"

"I can only tell you what I observe here from the office. Mr. Weiss has been an excellent employee ever since he was hired. Always on time, always sober. No one has uttered a disparaging remark about him." The clerk rolls back in his chair. "This is the first time he has been absent. I hope nothing untoward has happened to him."

"It's still early in the investigation. I need someone to identify a body found last night. Unfortunately, he fits the description. Do you have an address for next of kin?" Majewski won't feel satisfied until he has a victim's name.

The clerk spins in his chair and opens a file cabinet. Nimble fingers search through notecards.

"Here it is. Mr. Weiss lives—lived—with his mother on South Carey Street."

On his way to South Carey Street, Majewski passes through the slaughterhouse production floor. The sounds and smells of death dominate. It is cold, damp, and dark inside. Above the commotion, he can hear the bellow of a man shouting orders and insults at his workers.

Majewski stands behind a pillar and observes the workplace. At the heart of the operation is the foreman. Majewski is surprised to hear all the noise that comes out of such a fellow. A small man barely five feet tall, he would pass for a child if he didn't have a dark, unkempt beard and a bald head. His belly hangs over his pants, straining the suspenders that keep everything together. The foreman waddles more than walks and is vicious to both man and beast.

"Get these fucking carcasses out of here and on a hook. You lazy fucking bastard, get off your ass and get to work. Cram that union shit up your ass." A running monologue of command flows from the foreman.

"Excuse me. Detective Majewski, Baltimore Police. Can I ask you a few questions?" Majewski shows his badge.

"What about? I'm busy here." The foreman barely looks at the detective.

"Do you know Henry Weiss?"

"Weiss. That lazy piece of shit. You would think, for the size of him, you could get a pound of work out of him. I think he was shell-shocked during the war. He's just not all there … if you know what I mean." The foreman smirks. "Is he in trouble? He didn't show up for work."

"Is that like him, to not show up?" Majewski asks.

"No, he's dumb as a post, but he always shows up and on time. Most of these cocksuckers can't say the same." The foreman shouts that part at some workers.

"What about drinking? Did he have trouble with anyone here?" Majewski hopes for a motive to materialize.

"Not Henry. Don't get me wrong. I hate that piece of useless shit like my own kid, but he was never drunk and barely talked to anyone to get in trouble." The foreman keeps his glare moving around the work floor, looking to pounce at the first transgression.

"The boys tease him because he's quiet. You'd think after being in the war, he'd a fucked some of them French women. But he would get all flustered just asking for his paychecks from the office gal. And she's at least a hundred, the old bitch. That's when he would get some shit from the boys. Nothing worse than any of them got." The foreman looks at his watch and hints he's done.

"One more question. Do you know if he was religious? Where he went to church?" Majewski still has the dead man's pose on his mind.

"Religious—church! Who the fuck do you think you're talking to? What the fuck would I know about him going to church? That's enough. Go waste someone else's time." The foreman spins all five feet of himself around and walks away.

3. October 21, 1919, 5:45 pm: 245 South Carey St., Baltimore

Majewski walks with a hitch in his step. The damp air makes the bones in his hips grind against each other. He moves past the Baltimore & Ohio Railroad roundhouse and on to Carey Street. The cobblestones in the streets are laid out haphazardly, like the teeth of a jack-o-lantern. Brick sidewalks show more discipline, arranged in diagonal patterns. Even in the dreary cold weather, little old German women keep the white wooden steps spotless and the windows shining like mirrors, a tough job with all the dust and exhaust in the air.

That is, except for 245 S. Carey St. The front door has some holes about shin-high. The wooden steps are grey, and broken screens hang off their hinges. The windows look like a pair of sad eyes.

Majewski investigates the backyard. The garden has long been neglected. Trash piles look well established and create a fetid smell. The whole yard has the stink of decay about it. Feral cats scatter like leaves in the wind. Majewski pokes through the debris looking for—what? He is uncertain. Under the rotted porch, he clears a pile of leaves and is taken aback by what he finds, a miniature graveyard with tiny wooden crosses. Each cross has a name on it. Pierre, Madeleine, Louis, Antoinette, even a small cross inscribed *Henri*. Majewski is mystified by the discovery.

Majewski returns to the front of the house. Concerned that the door may not handle the force of the door knocker, he gently knocks. Paint chips tumble with each tap.

"Hello. Detective Majewski, Baltimore Police. Is anyone home?" He tries to peer through grime- encrusted windows. Knocks louder. "Hello!"

"Chrissake, I'm coming, hold your goddam horses." An old fat lady in a flannel housecoat, barely taller than the doorknob, answers. She blows out a lungful of cigarette smoke. "Who the hell are you?"

She gives Majewski the once over. He's wearing a long overcoat and bowler hat. His shoes are shined but look as if they had a rough day. He waves his badge as if it has magical powers. She is not impressed. "Fancy boy, huh."

"Sorry to bother you, Madam, but do you know where Henry Weiss may be?" Majewski is not looking forward to this conversation.

"That damn kid hasn't been home for a while. Leaving his old mother here alone." Mrs. Weiss takes a step back, a bit surprised. "Well, out with it, what did he do?"

"May I come in? I have something to tell you." Majewski doesn't wait for permission; he squeezes past the old lady into the narrow hallway.

His nose is immediately assaulted with the acrid smell of cat piss. He can't hide his disgust. In the sitting room, he can see six or seven cats on a scuffed-up couch. The room is bleak. Blankets and rags cover the windows, keeping the sunlight at bay. The place is a disheveled mess of old newspapers, liquor bottles, trash, and dirty dishes strewn across the floor. The wallpaper clings to the wall with the last of its glue. Yellow stains offer clues to a leaky roof, with cracks outlining future disaster.

"Henry has cats, most of them are outside, but a few sneak in." Mrs. Weiss offers a faint smile. "He just loves the kitties. Henry takes care of so many. He is always outside picking them up and petting them. It's cute in a sad way. I mean he's a big oaf, and they're so little in his hands. He's so gentle holding them like he's their momma. Feeding them like they were his kids. I tell him he is a fool for taking on so many, but he says, 'If I don't, who will?' He gave them all French names." She holds her hand up like a traffic cop. "But don't ask me who's who."

"Mrs. Weiss, you may want to sit down." Majewski realizes that finding a clean place to sit may be a tall order. His eyes begin to water. "Most of the cats are outside, you say. Interesting."

The old lady drops like an artillery shell into an overstuffed chair. Cat hair explodes off the upholstery. Her housecoat opens up as she lands, with modesty the casualty.

"Excuse me, ma'am, you're a bit ..." Majewski points to her fallen housecoat.

"Oh my, Mr. Ma ... I'm sorry." Mrs. Weiss attempts an embarrassed look. It's been a while since anyone has seen her below the neck.

16

"Majewski, Detective Majewski." His expression turns to concerned. "Those marks on your shoulders, where did they come from? If you don't mind my being inquisitive."

Majewski looks down at the old woman's hands, the backs of which bear marks the size of cigarette burns.

"Those marks on your hands, from the same source?" Majewski asks.

"Oh, those, they're old." Mrs. Weiss seems self-conscious. "That's all Henry's father left me before he went to Cuba—for the war. He never came back."

"I'm sorry. Died in combat, did he?" Majewski sees his job getting tougher.

"The bastard didn't die. Just never came back. He met a whore and lives in Havana. Where are my cigarettes?"

Mrs. Weiss gets up and rummages around looking for her smokes.

"You know Henry's much like his father. Not very smart. I don't mind telling you Henry can be a handful. Especially since he's come back from France. I think he saw things there that upset him." Mrs. Weiss leans in toward Majewski. "It's girls. I think the French girls were too bawdy for him. He used to tell the same joke he picked up in the army. 'What do you call a whore with two black eyes? A whore you had to tell twice.'"

Mrs. Weiss has a chuckle at her own expense. "To tell you the truth, I don't get it."

"Exactly what upset him?"

"The war had a bad effect on Henry. He was in artillery. Loud noises really bothered him. That's why yelling at him doesn't do any good. Just like his father. I mean, yelling at him didn't do any good either. Little things can get Henry angry. His temper got worse after the war."

She reaches up on a shelf and pulls off a medal in a glass picture frame. "They gave Henry a medal when he got hurt. They gave him other ones, but Henry did something with them. Don't ask me what."

"What did he do when he got angry? Did he ever hurt you?"

"Oh goodness, no. Henry would cover his ears and go outside to find a quiet place. That's when he would go play with his kitties. They seem to calm his nerves." Mrs. Weiss seems surprised by the question.

Majewski didn't know how to break in and deliver the news of Henry's death.

"The doctors told him he could never be a father. But I told him he didn't need to worry about having kids because he would always have me to take care of."

She looks at the medal with a small smile.

"He's a good boy. Always makes me breakfast, then dinner when he gets home. Besides, what woman would have him? He isn't exactly a catch. And I'm his mother saying that."

"Mrs. Weiss, there is something you should know." Majewski looks away. "Last night there was an incident in the park. The victim matches Henry's description."

The words float out and linger in the air, waiting to land with a thud. Mrs. Weiss stumbles back into her chair.

"The park? Last night? The park?" Mrs. Weiss tries to understand the location, its implications, Henry's condition. "It's not Henry. He's a good boy. He's probably still at work."

"Mrs. Weiss, he didn't show up at work. Where else would he go? Does he have friends?" Majewski wants to add, friends that aren't feral cats with French names. "Would you please come to the morgue so we can be sure?"

Majewski expects a rough time at the morgue. He's not disappointed. Mrs. Weiss goes into sobs of mourning, berating the deity that allowed this to happen to her sick baby. Other than identifying the body, there was little to learn. The pastor from St. Mary's makes the funeral arrangements.

Majewski plans a trip there to see if there is anything else that might explain what happened to Henry Weiss.

4: October 22, 1919, 4:20 pm: St. Mary's Church

"Father O'Donnell, here. Good to meet you." The pastor tamps out his cigarette and extends his hand to greet Detective Majewski. "I am so sorry to hear about Henry Weiss. I don't know if I can help you. He and his mother only show up on the holidays."

"Is there anything you can tell me that can help me understand why a man like Weiss went to the park at night?" Majewski asks the priest. "Did he ever confide in you?"

"Henry hadn't been to church much since he was young. I knew he was a troubled child. His parents were always fighting. That ended when the boy's father left for Cuba. Then, the mother started to drink more than usual."

The priest looks out the rectory window, searching for answers.

"Henry was quiet and big for his age. I think people expected more from him because they thought he was older than he was. As a nine-year-old altar boy, he was a head taller than the other boys."

"An altar boy?" Majewski thinks about the dead man's pose. Maybe there really was a religious bent to the crime.

"Yes, but not for long. Henry went to school here for a while. Before the father went to Cuba. He didn't make friends easily. He was a bit slow compared to the other kids. They picked on him a lot, even though he was so much bigger than everyone else. Henry just seemed defenseless against their teasing."

Father O'Donnell turns from the window and faces Majewski. The priest rocks on his feet. There seems to be something on his mind, something having a hard time coming out. The priest retreats back to the window and lets his gaze extend to the city skyline.

"May I ask you a question, Detective?" Father O'Donnell searches the sky for words that elude him.

"Sure, Father." Majewski steps closer to the desk.

"Why did you become a policeman?"

"After the war, I needed a job. Like anyone else."

"There are plenty of jobs. You seem intelligent." Father O'Donnell looks the detective over. He sees a clean-shaven man, a bit gray around the temples, of average height. His clothes hang on his slender frame just right. He looks more like a banker than a policeman. Each layer of clothing is well-pressed or laundered. He'd put money on Majewski being a former Calvert School boy and then a Gilman Country School "man."

"You could have chosen to be a doctor, a lawyer, an architect, maybe even…" Father O'Donnell extends his arms, displaying his office in the rectory.

"A priest."

"Maybe. We both like stiff collars."

Majewski instinctively adjusts his Windsor knot and can feel the razor edge of his starched collar cut across his neck.

The priest grins, then returns to the window searching for the words. "I think there are things about being a policeman that made you become one. I think you want to serve a higher power. In this case, the law. You believe in what you do—true?"

Majewski lets the words settle in and concedes.

"Priests believe in God's law. So we are much alike. Then there is the service to one's flock. You have a precinct and I, a parish."

The words start to come to the priest.

"We need to protect them from the evils in this world."

Majewski isn't sure where this conversation is going. He looks at his watch, a subtle hint that doesn't land.

"Both of us in our vocations see the frailties in our flocks. We just have different perspectives, so to speak. You're charged with prosecuting misdeeds and seeing to justice in this life. I need to offer forgiveness in this world to prepare souls for the next."

Father O'Donnell speaks in a hushed tone, as if he's in a confessional.

"Both our vocations are made up of men who share our desires."

The priest takes a long pause.

"*Desire* is an interesting word. Don't you think? It means simply what the heart wants. Our hearts, yours and mine, our desire, is to serve the higher power and protect our flocks."

Father O'Donnell closes his eyes. He wants to shut out the visions of the past, but they burn like a candle.

"But—there are men in our vocations stalked by temptation. Satan's in the shadows looking to bend and distort men's higher desires. He stands watching over each man's weak spot. Maybe a policeman needs some cash. Suddenly someone shows up and offers cash in exchange for a blind eye. Maybe he has a man's needs. A woman appears and trades her service for future favors."

Father O'Donnell drops his head and heaves a long sigh.

"Maybe it's not always a woman."

Words fall out in a whisper not meant to be heard. He's not satisfied by what he's saying.

"Is there something you're trying to tell me? Majewski prompts. "It's best just to be straight."

"Tell me, Detective, when you find a comrade who breaks the law, falls from grace, someone who has succumbed to temptation, is your first thought to ostracize him or try to save him, rehabilitate a lost soul?" The priest is still using confessional tones. "I know policemen rally around their own. It's natural. And so do we. We also protect our own."

The priest reaches for his cigarettes and lights one with nervous fingers. He takes a deep drag and lets the smoke circle around his head.

"You know, confession can be a wonderful thing. It can take a tremendous weight off the soul. I've heard thousands of confessions, from the petty to the horrifying. I keep each one tucked up here," the priest points to his head, smoke billowing like a crown of thorns, "and I'll take each one to the grave. Tell me, Detective, what do I do with these sins? They're not mine, yet I know. I gave the absolutions, I freed the sinner. Now the sins are mine to hold."

Majewski's pulse races.

"Each night I see the tawdry, the despicable, the violent images of sin play in my mind like a nickelodeon. I trade absolution for a few Hail Marys or a nice donation in the basket. Tell me, Detective, am I as corrupt as the women who work the park after dark?"

Majewski came into the rectory to ask a few questions. Now he is having a philosophical discussion with the parish pastor.

"Henry always appeared older than he was. Some found that confusing. I mean he seemed to some more mature than the other boys." Father O'Donnell searches for the right words.

"How is it that a nine-year-old boy, who was picked on for being slow," Detective Majewski asks, "seemed so mature?"

"Not I, you understand, but there were some here who became friendly with Henry. The hope was to protect him from the outside world. He showed great promise."

Father O'Donnell moves behind his desk as if needing protection.

Majewski shoots point blank at the priest. "Protection from what? What kind of promise? Was he filled with the Spirit?"

Father O'Donnell holds on to the back of his desk chair. "Sometimes—well, emotions and passions can—look, let's just say more was expected from Henry, but he was too young. He was like a large cherub, but not quite ready..."

"Not ready? Not ready for what? Holy Orders?"

"Look, it's all in the past. The problem was moved to another parish where temptations were less available."

Father O'Donnell knows his words are falling flat. There is no acceptable way of saying what needs to be said. Why did he say anything? There is no way to unburden himself without betraying his vows. With Henry's death, the priest prays the incident can pass into history, releasing him as well.

Detective Majewski forms an image of Henry Weiss's life. A poor kid with horrible parents, oversized, not very bright, torn by taunts and worse, betrayed by those who were supposed to protect his soul. Then shipped off to France to load artillery shells, only to be savagely wounded. At every turn, Henry was failed by everyone. Eventually left to die, cold and alone, with his pants around his ankles. No justice can make this right.

Majewski paces back and forth in front of the parish priest's desk.

"So now you pass the sin to me. You're right, my job is not to forgive, only to prosecute." Majewski's knuckles turn bone-white in his fists. "Yes, our perspectives are very different, Father."

"I don't care what you think." The priest moves to the defensive. "But Henry was loved here. Sometimes love can take unusual forms, so to speak. Sometimes love is not defined the same way for everyone. Sometimes..."

"Enough with your bullshit. I should come back here and throw the lot of you in jail." Majewski throttles his rage.

"Well, I'll tell you he was better off here than in the back alley with those hooligans and guttersnipes." Father O'Donnell trades contrition for self-righteousness. He waves at the window pointing down the street. "If you really want to know about Henry's life, go talk to them. They led him into

24

every form of temptation. They taught him foul language, how to steal, how to gamble. They tortured him because he was different. He was at least precious here, safe from them."

"He wasn't safe here." Majewski knew he had to leave, or he would be a criminal himself. "I'm not done here. I'll be back, and I will make sure justice happens in this life and not the after. Thank you, Father."

5: October 22, 1919, 5:30 pm: Napoleon's Army

It's getting dark. A miserable cold mist turns to miserable light rain. Majewski pulls his collar up and holds tight to his scarf. His hips ache. Pain shoots down his legs. The sidewalk bricks get sparse. He searches for signs of illicit life in the alleys along Washington Street. The smell of burning trash leads him to those he's looking for. A gang of half a dozen kids pitch scraps of wood into a metal drum to burn. It's hard to keep the count straight as the kids come and go at a spirited pace; as best he can tell, the ages run from about nine to sixteen or seventeen. These poorly clothed street urchins remind him of characters out of a Dickens novel. Dirty, torn, ill-fitted rags would describe the apparel of the best-dressed.

A thrown bottle shatters at Majewski's feet. Not the greeting he hoped for. He walks toward the gang, refusing to show intimidation. He's survived the Kaiser's ammunition during the Great War. Street punks from Pigtown aren't the ones to do him in. He warms his hands over the fire. The gang circles round him in silence. The bigger kids make it clear they have knives. Majewski lets his overcoat fall open so everyone clearly knows he has a Smith & Wesson .38 special.

"There are more of us." A big kid with wild red hair threatens the detective.

"Doesn't matter. I'll be aiming at you."

Surprised, the red-haired kid looks around for backup. None is offered. The circle breaks up and turns to another kid standing on a stage made of wooden crates. Majewski needs to see who demands the attention.

Majewski guesses the kid to be about thirteen. A moth-riddled wool cap is pulled over his eyes, letting big drops of rain drain. A dark duster keeps him dry, but the ripped pockets don't offer any help. His shoes look like worn-out pass-me-downs. Jumping off the crate stage, the kid walks up to the detective with the swagger of a hoodlum chieftain.

"Who are you to walk into my alley and share my fire?" The kid looks Majewski in the eye, though he's at least a foot shorter than the detective.

"Free country. I go as I please." Majewski looks down to trade cold stares. "Who are you to claim this alley?"

"They call me Napoleon. This is my empire. From the gutter to the dead end. And this is my army."

Raindrops form streams of grime to wash down the little general's face. He assesses Majewski.

"Now—who are you to come here, unless you're looking to lose your wallet. Or those nice new boots." The diminutive emperor turns his back on Majewski.

"I'm a detective."

"Olie—Smoke." Napoleon snaps his fingers. One of the younger kids responds with a cigarette.

"A detective? What have we done to take up a detective's valuable time? We only break windows and commit petty theft."

Napoleon lights up and tosses the matchstick away with a flourish. He walks up to Majewski and opens the policeman's overcoat, satisfied to see a badge with the revolver.

"You're still going to shoot that one, right?" Napoleon laughs, pointing—cigarette in hand—to the red-haired kid Majewski threatened to take down. The gang laughs on cue, in unison.

"Listen, mister, I'm not sure what you're looking for. We're vandals and pickpockets. Maybe I can help you with a lucky number. Sometimes we manage to find a case of tomatoes or whiskey that falls off a truck. You in the market? But if you're looking for a boy whore? You and your gun and badge need to try another alley. Or go up to the Druid Hill Park by the zoo. I hear you can fuck a boy whore or an elephant."

Giggles erupt from the boys. Napoleon has a boy's face scattered with peach fuzz. It's his eyes that betray a dangerous person waiting for his body to catch up.

"You should know that."

"It's this park I wanted to talk to you boys about." Majewski keeps his eye on Napoleon and his sixth sense on the gang. "Do you know what goes on there after dark?"

"No. Does the boogeyman come out?" Napoleon takes a long drag off his cigarette. He keeps a poker face.

"Maybe. How about Henry Weiss? Anyone know him?" Majewski strikes a nerve with the gang. No one says a word, but silent messages shoot back and forth.

"Henry? What did that idiot do?"

Napoleon only knows there was a murder. The victim's name hasn't been released. "Did he get that guy in the park a few nights ago?"

"Do you think he could have done it?"

Majewski keeps Napoleon in the dark. The gang circles around looking like each has a theory. But it's clear nobody says anything without Napoleon's permission.

Napoleon takes his time thinking about what to say about Henry Weiss. His army looks as if the troopers are ready to break ranks and spill it to the detective.

"Yea. I think so." Napoleon says.

One of the kids speaks out. "That guy should be locked up like a lunatic."

"What do you mean? I hear he was a nice fellow." Majewski is caught off guard.

"Hell no!"

"Bullshit!"

"Asshole!"

The gang emits a chorus of character references. Napoleon holds his hand up. Everyone shuts up.

"I'll tell you about the last time we saw that lunatic." Napoleon offers, "But it'll cost you."

One of Napoleon's lieutenants steps up, and takes his hat off, shoves it toward Majewski.

The detective reaches into his pocket and pulls out a two-bit coin. He shows it to the gang, making everyone get a look before he flips it into the hat.

"I thought you said you were a detective. Is that the best you can pay for information?" The little emperor has a cocksure manner. "You think all we do is play tiddlywinks and jacks?"

Majewski laughs, recognizing his match, and finds another coin to toss into the hat.

"So, tell me about Mr. Weiss?" Majewski asks.

"Henry has been the neighborhood patsy since before we were born. Our dads, uncles, brothers—everyone—used to pick on him. He's always been an easy mark. It's like a tradition." Napoleon explains the Weiss lineage of larceny. "I think that kept him alive. He was a source of money, the golden duck or whatever, so no one ever did him in—even when he deserved it."

"Deserved it? What did he do to deserve anything?"

"Henry Weiss could be a problem when he got loaded. So they'd play him right to the edge. Then give him a good slap or kick in the ass and send him on his way."

"We knew it was payday and Henry would be walking this way. He likes to play cards and craps but hates to lose. So we don't let him play too often. But we were short on cash and let him play. He was grand when he was winning. So we offered him a bit of whiskey that fell off a truck." Napoleon puffs on his cigarette and blows blue smoke straight up from his jutted lower lip. "I don't think losing got him mad this time. He always lost. But the boys were giving him a harder time than usual."

"Why was that?" Majewski inquires.

"Not sure. Sometimes the boys just play rough." Napoleon shrugs.

"It was funny. The more he lost, the more he drank and the madder he got." One of the kids spoke up, grinning.

"It was the name-calling that pissed him off," Napoleon asks his infantry. "What did you guys call him?"

"You know. Limp Dick—Momma's Boy." The grinning boy is happy to answer.

"That's when Weiss started getting hinky, that and losing all his money." Napoleon takes over the narrative. "He was pretty ossified, stumbling around, swinging at everyone, tipped over the fire, could have burned the block down. He kept swigging away from our bottle of whiskey. It was like watching an ape going wild."

"Was he always like this?"

Majewski wonders if this is a tall tale or the truth. This is not the same person he has been learning about.

"No. Most times he just mopes away. I never saw him this off his head." Napoleon stays on course. "But we know how to take care of him."

"How?" Majewski can only imagine the solution issued by the grammar school dictator.

"Tell him about Whitey." There is wide agreement from the gang. "Show him."

Whitey is pushed forward. Black-and-Blue would be a more appropriate nickname. The kid's face is bruised. His britches are ripped, showing off scrapes on his knees.

"Yea. Whitey ran his mouth to Henry, and his legs didn't run fast enough to get away with it. Henry grabbed him and gave him a good beating and dragged him all over the alley like a rag doll." Napoleon says. "What tipped him over the edge? What did you say?"

"You can't fuck your momma with a soggy sausage." Whitey meekly answers, still afraid of another beating if Henry gets wind of this.

"'You can't fuck your momma with a soggy sausage.' I'm going to fuck your momma with my sausage, chrissake." Napoleon gives Whitey a disappointed look. "That sent him over? Weiss must have really been drunk."

"And nobody tried to stop it?"

"Have you seen the size of that son of a bitch?" The red-haired kid calls out. Loyalty runs only so deep.

"How do you know about his," Majewski wonders how an intimate detail like that gets around, "eh, sausage?"

A big kid answers. "Little Olie's half-sister is a floozy, and she said Henry couldn't do what he paid for."

The gang titters like the bunch of children they are. Olie nods, unsure what he's agreeing with.

"Anyway. Weiss hates loud noises, so we banged the trash lids on the bricks. He grabbed his ears and a half-full bottle of our whiskey and ran off," Napoleon says.

"Where do you think he went?" Majewski is still trying to balance the two different images of Henry Weiss.

"Who knows? He kept yelling 'I'm a man.' Which only made everyone laugh. Maybe he went up to the park to try to fuck a whore, maybe he went home to his shitty cats." Napoleon offers two scenarios.

"Cats?"

"Yea, cats. Look under the porch and dig around. Everything you need to know about Henry Weiss is buried there."

Napoleon thinks for a moment.

"To answer your first question again. Yeah, I think Henry could have killed that guy in the park."

6: October 22, 1919, 8:45 pm: Majewski goes to the diner

A heavy rain chases Majewski limping into a diner to wait out the storm. Ceiling fans spin slow and silent, turning the air into a hazy slush of tobacco smoke and grease. The detective sees he's not the only one escaping the wet and cold. There are two booths in the back crowded with women. Not so strange to see—until he realizes the group is made up of blue-uniformed suffragists and garishly clad women who patrol the park in the wee hours. Odd bedfellows, to say the least.

He sits at the counter within earshot of the women. Bits and pieces of conversation drift over to him.

"It's our time. We can vote soon, and we can change the world."

"It's our bodies and no man can say what we do with them."

"You women perform a service like any other. You should unionize."

Hot flashes from the open grill hit Majewski in the face. The heat feels good. Smiling, Majewski orders a cup of coffee and a slice of apple pie.

Hot black coffee warms his insides and gets his mind back to figuring out his case. Crimes like these are a dime a dozen in the city. Another body added to the ledger won't make much difference. Majewski knows he won't be given much more time to find the perpetrator. Was it a single act, a business transaction gone wrong? Or was this the act of a gang preying on the vulnerable? If it's a gang, then there will be more to follow. Either way, he has to resolve things soon. There's no shortage of crimes in Baltimore to write about.

All life being a gamble, apparently Weiss had placed all his chips on a number that was never his to lose. What Majewski has a hard time figuring out is how Weiss was able to be a quiet, diligent worker and dutiful son, caring for stray cats as surrogate family, then be a guy who was a ticking bomb waiting to explode. When did fate etch Henry Weiss's name on that ice pick? At birth, to parents who never really loved him? The priests who stole his youth? The army that left him half a man? The gangs that used him for extortion? Grim fate had stalked Weiss in the park's shadows, talons drawn, and finished him.

"... And the best part will be when the 18th Amendment becomes the law of the land. Sobriety sisters, imagine, no more drunken husbands or drunken fathers. We do have power. We have only to take it."

Majewski turns to see the voice that interrupts his thoughts. A tall blonde suffragist—for the news piece, he'll call her a suffragette—stands on her chair speaking to the other women. The professional women listen to the rhetoric with passing interest.

"Ladies, it's our time. We have but to ask for what we want. Now, what do we want?"

"I wouldn't have to do this shit if we could make some decent dough at one of the factories or slaughterhouses. Can we get that?" An older working woman in a fake fur coat speaks out.

"Doesn't Wilson want doctor visits for everyone, even us?" A concerned young courtesan of the shadows asks. She won't tell anyone, but she has a problem that can't be washed away with vinegar.

"I'd be happy fucking a man indoors, how about a nice brothel with clean sheets?" A wise old hen with a big bosom and plunging neckline chimes in, followed by a chorus of laughter. "That would be lovely."

"Maybe we can help you find another occupation so you wouldn't need to submit to a man's selfish pleasures." The blonde suffragist has hopes for higher aspirations.

The diner doors swing open, letting in the rain and a new round of customers.

"Hey Lou, set me and the boys up with some ham and eggs." A big fellow, broad as he is tall, bellows as if he owns the place. Three other men enter with him and shake off the rain, splashing the suffragists in the next booth.

Majewski laughs to himself while he observes the room and can only imagine the uniforms coming in to restore order.

The big loud one calls out, "Lou, send some beers over too."

"You got it, Gus. Already under the tap." The counter guy knows his regulars.

"Atta boy, buddy."

The men light up cigarettes—all except Gus. He ignites a foot-long stogie.

At the suffragists' table, the women start coughing. Gus notices and puffs like a coal-burning factory on overtime.

"Excuse me, sir." The tall blond suffragist approaches the table of men. "Would you be gentlemen and refrain from smoking in front of the ladies?"

The request almost kicks the cigar out of Gus's mouth. He is beyond disbelief that some strange woman would dare speak to him that way. Majewski sits on his stool as if it were a box seat at the Hippodrome, taking in the melodrama.

"Ladies? Ladies? I don't see no ladies. I see some dressed up twats and some whores. But ladies. Not one." Gus stands up for a better look at the female horde. The suffragists huddle together for protection while the more worldly women form a phalanx readying for action.

"I fought in the war. I earned my cigar. While I was fighting in trenches watching my friends die in the fucking mud—you and your cunt friends in Congress were taking away my right to drink, and now you're going to vote like men. Holy shit, what was it for?" He puts his cigar back in his mouth and re-lights. "Jesus, what's next, letting the niggers eat in here? Christ."

"Kick him in the balls," one of the vamps suggests.

"Try it." Gus takes a menacing step toward the blonde, and that's when Majewski becomes an actor in this melodrama.

"That's enough. Let's leave the ladies alone. Ladies, can we keep a still tongue?" Majewski tries to be a diplomat.

"Ain't you the dandy, telling us what to do. Piss off. You look like you never worked a day in your life and you don't know shit about the war. So you don't have a right to talk to me. Go mind your own business." Gus looks Majewski over and stands belly to gut.

"I know more about the war than you'd like to hear." Battlefield memories are still open wounds to Majewski. "And tossing morons like yourself in jail I find pleasure, not work. So I guess you're right. I never worked a day." Majewski opens his coat to show his hardware of copper and steel. "Now sit your ass down and act like a gentleman or get run in for disorderly conduct and whatever else I think of along the way."

Gus and the boys settle into their seats.

"Would it be all right to have a beer, if we don't smoke, Miss?" one of the men asks politely—or sarcastically. Whichever, the threat of authority has had an impact.

"And we won't cuss." He crosses his heart and holds his hand up in an oath. "Swear to Christ."

"Ladies, I think it's the most you can ask of hardworking men." Majewski turns back to the women for their answer.

There are grudging head nods from the suffragists. The women from the park grunt in more audible agreement.

Gus takes a seat and puts out his stogie. "Bullshit. Fine."

"I normally run when I see a cop. But you seem swell." A chubby lady, whose stock in trade bulges up front, thanks Majewski. "Maybe you'd like one on the house?"

"Thank you, Officer," the blonde suffragist leader chimes in.

"Detective, Madam. Detective Majewski," Majewski tips his bowler.

"Yes, Detective. Thank you, but I think we can take care of ourselves from here." The suffragist wants to return to her speechmaking.

"Speak for yourself, sister." One of the working ladies walks up to the suffragist leader. It must have taken gallons of whiskey and bales of tobacco to give her a voice that gravelly. "In fact, why don't you go find someone who wants to hear you yak. We could use a good man."

The lead suffragist frowns and takes a seat with her colleagues. She and Gus are no longer the center of attention.

"I'm Alice, but my street name is Velvet, cause I'm so fucking soft."

Majewski gives Alice a look-over. If he were a sculptor and could chisel away time, he'd find a statuesque young girl. Time has created its own cruel version of her.

"You know me and the girls here work the park, and we could use a man to keep an eye on things for us." Alice runs her hands over Majewski's chest. "I'm sure there are things we can do to help one of the city's best."

Majewski blushes. It's been a long time since he felt a woman's lingering touch. He still hasn't gotten used to his wife and son living in Roanoke with another man. The idea of her under another man, makes him nauseous. Between the army and police force, he has been living like a monk, depriving himself of carnal and social pleasures as punishment for a failed marriage. The army gives out medals for injuries earned in battle; eventually they heal, and you're left with a limp or fear of loud noises. But the lacerations of the heart never close. The heart bleeds until it's only a muscle pumping in a void. No medals come from these wounds—just sad poetry.

"Rose here does a specialty that leaves most men speechless. But I bet you're not most men." Alice is still trying to sell her idea. Rose lifts her skirt to show off an exquisitely round bottom and gives it a sultry grind.

Majewski can only imagine what that specialty could be and manages a small smile. Instinctively he looks around to see if Satan is lurking, or worse, if he might be seen by someone he knows.

"We have a good thing at the park. There are only a few of us, we're close to the slaughterhouse guys and the swells from Bolton Hill. So far we've barely been noticed by the gangs, but the Italians are looking in our direction. We could use a cop on our side. If you don't want Rose's ass, maybe you need a man or maybe just straight old-fashioned cash?" Alice becomes Satan's agent, poking for Majewski's weakness.

Majewski allows his mind to wander. Even knowing what manner of woman stands in front of him, he falls for the glamour of sex. Images, perverse and sensual, fill his imagination. His curiosity creeps under Rose's skirt, haunting and exciting. But like any good monk, he purges and banishes his half-formed notions to the dark shadows of his mind where they belong. He doubts he'll be running to Father O'Donnell to confess impure thoughts any time soon.

"Do you think it was the Italians who did the business in the park the other night?" That would explain the ice pick in the throat. Seems like a Sicilian thing to do. Majewski steers his mind back on track.

"Could be, but I think it was more likely that bitch who works under the statue," Alice speculates. "The pick in the throat sounds more like her calling card. She's always getting into a fight with the johns."

"How so?" Majewski tilts his head to try to understand.

"She has an insane rule about nobody talking. She has a dinner bell for her men to ring. Just don't say anything, dear god. She has the temper of the devil." Alice holds her hands up in surrender and laughs.

"Does everyone have a spot in the park to work?"

"Not really," Alice instructs. "We walk about but give each other some room to work. But that rotten bitch wouldn't let anyone near her precious statue."

"Do you have a name?" This case is starting to fall into place. The suspect just needs to be apprehended, tried, and sentenced.

"No. We call her Mrs. Bells, because of her dinner bell. Not very clever, but fuck her, we don't like her, she's a foreigner, she's one of those who brought the big plague, we don't want her here." The fair weather in Alice's face changes to a storm. "You'll know who she is by the scar on her face."

7: October 23, 1919, 12:00 am: Searching the Weiss backyard

Tomorrow night Majewski will plan the suspect's apprehension. Nothing really complicated about arresting a single trollop. She just needs to hold up her end and show for work. But tonight there is one more stop to make. Something Napoleon said sticks a thorn in Majewski's paw: "Everything you need to know about Henry Weiss is under the porch."

Even at this late hour, the lights are on at 245 Carey Street. Majewski knocks on the door. There is no answer. He tries to peer through the window, but the grime makes it opaque. With some spit and a rub with his handkerchief, he peers in and sees Mrs. Weiss.

She's in her chair, still as death. Dead? Majewski thinks maybe so—until he hears her snores rattling the windows. On the table next to her chair, Majewski sees a bottle of Calvert Rye, a tumbler half full, and a cigarette burned down to a stub in the ashtray. He takes it upon himself to go into the yard. It's dark, and the footing is dangerous from all the trash. Some moonlight escapes cloud cover, illuminating the porch enough to see. Majewski strikes up a matchstick to see deeper underneath the porch.

Seeing the grave marked *Henri*, Majewski makes that the logical place to start. He finds a rusty claw hammer with a splintered wooden handle. Perfect for the task at hand. The match flames out and Majewski begins digging in the dark. He uses the claw of the hammer as a hoe, pulling the dirt apart in furrows. Only a few inches down, in front of the cross, he finds something. Preparing for the worst, that being a decaying cat, he's surprised to discover a metal box. Pulling it out into the moonlight, he looks it over.

There's no lock, only rusty hinges keeping the lid in place. Majewski pries with his fingers but can't get the lid to budge. He puts the hammer's claw to use and forces the box open.

There's no cat. Just stuff from Henry's life. Small things like baby shoes, a baptism certificate, then the real surprise. Battle ribbons from the war, Chateau-Thierry and Belleau Wood. Two battles in France that Pershing led. Majewski should know. He was at both actions and had a horse blown from under him at Belleau Wood. American and French forces pushed back the Germans at tremendous cost. Ammonia from spent ammunition is forever burned in his nostrils. The feeling in his stomach when the horse disappeared from under him still hasn't gone away. The last thing Detective Stanley Majewski sees before he falls asleep is the memory of things he wants to forget. Pain medication for the broken hip and bashed knees has become part of his daily ritual.

Now he finds that Weiss, this wreck of a man, is linked to him in a unique brotherhood. Weiss's unit must have been walloped. Old soldiers never talk about their battles. Words can't define the experience. It's that far beyond what anyone can explain. Images of chaos and death fill their brains, but there is no language for them. Even poetry fails. It's life lived at its most primal and savage level. The will to survive supersedes every other thought.

Shuffling through the box yields another surprise, one that softens Majewski's dour face. It's a photograph of Weiss in full dress uniform. Sitting on his lap is a beautiful young woman with long hair neatly done up in a French braid. Her dress is simple but stylish. Henry wears a smile that transcends his reality and his fate. His big hands wrap around the woman's small waist. His huge arms envelop her. Maybe there was a time in this poor wretch's life when he knew happiness? There is nothing written on the back of the photo, no date, no name. Just as well. Majewski wants to think this was a good experience for Weiss. God knows all the others were horrors.

He strikes another match and goes back into the cemetery. He picks the nearest grave before the flame extinguishes. Again the soft dirt yields under the hammer. He digs a bit deeper, hoping upon hope that he will find memorabilia of another lost love. Instead of a metal box, he finds a cloth with something in it. He works around the fabric as if he were excavating an Egyptian pharaoh. Majewski pulls the cloth bag out. At this point he's not hopeful it will hold artifacts from a past girlfriend.

He's right. It's the remains of a cat, stiff, fur dried out, bugs crawling out in panic. Nothing more than one would expect from a dead cat buried under the porch in a bag. Except for one thing.

"Oh, shit." The words tumble out of Majewski's mouth.

Majewski lights another match and exhumes another cat.

"Dear God."

Another match, another cat. It doesn't take long for the pattern to play out. There's no reason to keep digging.

Majewski shakes his head in disbelief. His respectable suit is covered with mud. Who was Henry Weiss? "Henry?" Majewski looks at the hammer in his hand and drops it in horror.

None of the feral cats had met a natural demise. Each cat had had its skull smashed.

An Angel and Demon Walk into a Bar

When is the story of a person's life written? At birth, a book of golden promises in waiting, or at death, the accounting of sins? Is it etched in the stone of time, or is it random numbers spinning on the wheel of fortune? Maybe each life is a billiard ball rolling along, bashing off the bumpers and into other balls. Perhaps it's a game of chance played by an angel and demon using mortal currency. Hit or stick, heaven or hell, a roll of the dice—salvation or damnation.

Every story has a beginning. This one started the moment the demon struck the cue ball, hurtling it toward a rack of mortal spheres. Stripes and solids ricocheted across a green baize, some finding a pocket, others destined to play it out to the end. The war in Europe was a game of chance. The demon chalked his stick. He took aim and sent the cue ball shooting into the abyss. It landed as an artillery shell, a flash of light, exploding in a trench in Flanders, scattering the destinies of men. Somewhere, lost in the night terrors, somewhere among the deaths, reason and humanity ran like refugees.

1: May, 1916: West Ireland

The Easter troubles of Dublin might as well be a thousand miles and a century away. Out here in the West, it's peaceful. What happens in the big city occurs in the newspapers, not out here. This is paradise, Tír na nÓg.

The pond is a mirror. The reflection holds the sun, blue sky, and cumulus clouds while the rowboat passes through it like a dream. Two young lovers drift with the breeze. The water licks the hull of their boat. The girl lets her hand trail in the water. She weaves her fingers, creating patterns in their wake. She looks at her young man, beguiled by his wavy black hair, how his slender hands slide along the guitar's neck. His voice is tender. He recites poems as if they were prayers. It's his eyes that capture her most. They're the color of a tormented sea.

"Danny, I wish today could last forever." The young girl feels the sun on her face. She lays her head in his lap, listening to him sing.

"*She bid me to take life easy, as the grass grows on the weirs, But I was young and foolish, and now I am full of tears.*" Danny strums the last chord and takes a nip from the bottle of whiskey. "Ah, you're a silly thing. We need to take love easy like Yeats says."

Falling in love with Danny is as natural as breathing.

"Dear Helen, I love you mad, but I want to go see the world. Come with me." Danny strums the guitar. "We don't need this. After the war, there will be a wave of peace that knows no bounds. Rome, St. Petersburg, Madrid. I want to write about them all."

"What is wrong with wanting the sun on your face, lying next to your true love, drifting without a care in the world?" Danny's strength of heart and dreams is contagious, but Helen wants him to herself, here in Ireland.

"Nothing, but the world is a big place, and Ireland is little. I want to see it all. New York, Boston, San Francisco, Montreal, Quebec. They are places waiting to hear my poems, to hear me sing."

"Isn't it enough to be the fine poet of West Sligo? I'll admit, I love to watch you dance. I know that's not what ladies are supposed to say." Helen smiles. "But nobody wants to hear you sing."

"I am surrounded by critics and assassins." Danny clutches his heart in a mock mortal wound, then taps his feet. "No, it's not enough. I want to conquer Sligo and Donegal. Then Dublin will lay laurels at my feet. I want Yeats, Joyce, Wilde to marvel at my art. After that who knows?" Danny laughs at his own arrogance. "I want to write about these other places, so other Irishmen know there's a huge world. A world that doesn't give a shit about kings and Kaisers."

"Let's not talk about them. I want you to sing me another song. Something happy!" Helen pretends to throw a tantrum, stamping her feet on the wooden hull.

"I'm sorry. It's just so…" Danny is at a loss for words.

Through not-quite-closed eyes, Helen watches Danny row, his shoulders moving under his white shirt, his forearms bare. She imaginges those arms holding her tight while they dance and if, when, later, they. . . A thrill of pleasure stabs her, makes her gasp, snaps her eyes wide open.

"Are you feeling a chill?" Danny asks.

"Are you daft? A chill on a day as fine as this?" The slight edge to her voice is intended for herself, a rebuke for her impure thoughts.

Eyes fully shut, Helen mentally reads the poem Danny left on her window sill this morning.

I'll build a cottage in a dell

Where in sweetest harmony

You, my lovely one, and me

Will evermore and longly dwell

And I will keep thee safe from pain

Till Gabriel sounds his trump again.

She knows its grammar and rhythm are a bit shaky. She knows there's no such word as "longly." She knows it is a marriage proposal. She knows what her answer will be.

Her mind rehearses how the afternoon will unfold. After a bit of picnicking he'll say the poem aloud, perhaps adding a line or two about the cottage filling with their children. He'll ask her to be his wife. He'll want to know if he has her permission to ask her father for her hand.

Helen grins at her da's predictable response. "Well, lad, you're a bit too bookish, but sure you're the reason every kid in the parish can stand before any man, woman, or child and recite the multiplication tables and throw in a poem for good measure." Her father secretly admires Danny for teaching the parish children in the rectory, and he openly admires Danny's keeping the fancy Harriss carriages shiny and running well. "You're no narrow-back, lad. You'll keep Helen well, and children too." Helen can almost hear the words being grumbled around her da's clay pipe.

The revelry of the moment is shattered by a harsh voice.

"Oy, oy. Bring that boat in." A British soldier commands the young lovers.

Helen sits up, bewildered. Danny grabs an oar for defense.

"Bring that boat in now, or I will shoot." The soldier has his rifle raised and aimed. He's joined by four others. Each soldier has his rifle at the ready as they spread out along the pond's bank. "Don't think. Just follow orders and bring the boat in."

"Danny, what do we do?" Helen quivers in fear.

"I don't think we have much choice." Danny's stomach knots.

Helen takes her place at the back of the boat. Danny moves to the middle and rows toward the bank.

"Good thinking, lad." The ruddy-faced soldier has sergeant stripes and is very comfortable in command of his men. "I want that boat searched."

Danny captains his boat up on the grassy bank and the soldiers swarm on them. They grab Helen and toss her out. Danny is gripped by two soldiers who lead him to a tree. The soldiers throw everything out of the boat, drag it farther on shore, and flip it over.

"No contraband, sir. Just these two kids," a soldier with the name Wainwright embroidered on his uniform tells the sergeant. "And some whiskey, bread, and cheese. Sir."

"Good. Let me see that whiskey." The sergeant walks over to the capsized boat and puts his foot on it. He gives it a shake, checking its structural integrity. He removes his gun belt and drops it by the stern. He wipes his brow with his arm. Wainwright hands him the bottle of whiskey. The sergeant pulls the cork out with his teeth and spits it out at Danny's feet. At the sergeant's head nod, the soldiers know what to do.

"Neely, Paddy. Contain the prisoner." The Sergeant points to Danny. "Stephens, take the point."

Neely lashes Danny's hands behind his back and throws him to the ground. Paddy drags him to the base of the tree. They position him in front of the boat.

Paddy, whose God-given name, Dougherty, is stitched to his uniform, grunts every time he hears "Paddy" followed by a demeaning order. This time it's to strap a belt around Danny's neck and lash him to the tree.

"How do you people swallow this piss?" The sergeant takes a swig of the whiskey and spits it out. He takes another gulp and passes it to Wainwright. "Pass it around to the lads."

Wainwright downs a mouthful and passes it along the pecking order.

"Slow down, they've already drunk half the bottle."

"How dare you? How dare you? Come out here for a picnic, when we have men dying in the war. And this is how you say thanks. Picnics and bloody rebellion." The sergeant, a thick, short man, bred for working in the Welsh coal mines, gets face to face with Danny.

"I didn't think a picnic was disrespectful." Danny is confused. He has no way to understand the rage in the soldier's heart.

"Shut up. First rule. No talking." The sergeant sticks his forefinger in Danny's face. He looks over at Helen. "That's a fine little tart you have. You fucking people couldn't plan a parade. Rebellion—my ass." The sergeant laughs. His patriotic fire burns hot. "Neely, give me that."

The sergeant takes control of the whiskey and drains the bottle. The whiskey accelerates the fury in his heart. A disappointed Paddy catches the empty bottle.

"I know just how you can say thank you to these gentlemen. We spent a year slogging about in Flanders. Ireland was supposed to be easy. Then this happens. Bastards can't be trusted." The sergeant signals for Neely to bring Helen over to the boat. "I think the young lady would consider it an honor to pleasure the king's men. Thank them for their service."

Danny flails against the belt strapped around his throat. He's unable to move, unable to defend Helen.

The sergeant looks around for witnesses in the hills. Confident he is lord and master of this little part of the world, he passes judgment on rebellious Irish youth.

"Besides we all know your women are whores. Catholic fucking whores." The sergeant makes another gesture, and the horror begins to play out in front of Danny. "What's another cock or two jammed in her? Eh?"

Wainwright and Neely throw Helen down on the boat's slimy wet hull. Her beautiful white linen picnic outfit is stained algae green. They grab her by the arms and hold her down. The sergeant stands behind her and tears her skirt off.

"New rule. Face away from me. I don't want to see you. You're nothing more than a fucking sheep that can't shed a sweater." The sergeant amuses himself by degrading Helen.

Danny screams. The belt cuts into his throat as he fights against the restraints. Helen receives a backhand across her face.

"Please, not this," Helen cries.

"I said no talking." Another backhand.

The demon whispers in the sergeant's ear. Here's the chance to avenge the injustice of it all. All he has to do is slam himself into this pretty young miss, and he'll be requited. The sergeant agrees with the demon. An enraged penis emerges from his trousers. The sergeant pumps all his rage and sense of injustice into Helen. She slumps, sobbing, across the bottom of the boat. The demon laughs, still holding the sergeant's wrath in his hand.

"You nasty bitch! I find the one virgin in this bloody country. Look at my uniform. I look like I've been shot. Bloody hell," the sergeant roars. Even after his release, his hatred burns at full flame. "Wainwright. Set up and be served for king and country."

Compliant, Wainwright steps behind Helen. Put off by the mess, he pours water from his canteen to clean off her rear end.

"No need to ruin two uniforms, eh." Wainwright, a good soldier, does his business for king and country as ordered.

"Stop. Please," Helen screams in protest and sobs in pain. Danny's eyes are wide open in horror.

"Hey, shut up. I said no talking." The sergeant feints another backhand. "I don't want to tell you one more time."

"Stephens, what's your problem?" The sergeant spots dissension in his ranks.

The sergeant walks over to his subordinate and sneers at him.

"Stephens, step up! It's your turn." The sergeant is more concerned about his orders being followed than about the scruples of a private.

"No thank you, Sir." Stephens turns away from Helen and his commander.

"I gave you an order. Now step up." The sergeant speaks slowly and forcefully.

Stephens puts his head down and walks toward Helen. Standing behind her, the soldier, a blue-eyed lad still in his teens, looks up at his squad leader. He bends down and picks up Helen's torn skirt and hands it to her.

"With respect, sir. I was conscripted to kill the enemy, not rape country girls," Stephens replies.

The sergeant pounces like an animal and swipes the pistol off Stephens' belt. He storms over to Danny. He cocks the hammer and aims it at Danny's head.

"You have a choice. You fuck that Irish whore, or I'll shoot this Fenian rebel in the head." The sergeant is demonic. This isn't an ethical debate. The issue is command and obedience. His orders must be carried out as if they are spoken by God.

"Sergeant, sir. They are just kids out for some craic. Let them be." Paddy immediately regrets interfering. "I can't see this either. It's not right. I'm from this county. These are my people, not the enemy."

"Outrageous! I will have the two of you court-marshaled for insubordination." The sergeant points the pistol at Stephens. His face is red, the veins in his head ready to explode. "You do as ordered, soldier. Now fuck that bitch."

"No, sir." Stephens raises his rifle and aims it at his superior.

Paddy is as confused as the rest of the squad but realizes the Irishmen are outnumbered in the debate.

Helen regains her balance and comes to terms with what is happening. At her feet is the Sergeant's gun belt, his pistol still holstered. She looks over at Danny, strapped defenseless to the tree.

"Put that fucking gun down, or I will shoot you." The sergeant takes aim at Stephens' head and gives his last ultimatum.

The two English soldiers watch, trying to understand what is happening.

"I will not" is the last thing Stephens says. The sergeant pulls the trigger. Stephens falls dead before the shot's echo stops ringing in the hills.

A storm of disbelief sweeps through the squad like a storm.

"Jesus, Sergeant." Wainwright stands in shock. "You shot one of our own men."

Neely deals with the incident differently. He drops his gear and immediately runs as fast as he can, disappearing into the high grasses along the pond's bank.

Helen slides off the boat and picks the gun out of the sergeant's holster. She's never seen one before, never mind fired one. The soldiers are too distracted to notice her take the offensive. As quietly as she can, she comes up behind the sergeant. Danny can only observe and pray for her.

Shaking like a blade of grass in the wind, Paddy aims his rifle at his commander.

"I'm going to blow your fucking head off." The sergeant spits as he yells at the private.

"No." Helen holds the gun pointed at the sergeant. It's heavy and awkward in her hands. She keeps it close, bracing it against her body. The gun shakes. She pulls the hammer back until it clicks. It's the sickening sound no soldier wants to hear. The sergeant takes a step back and laughs at what he sees.

"Oh dear God. The Irish whore has a gun. Put that down, Miss, before you get hurt. After I take care of this traitor, I'll be ready for another go." The sergeant still has his gun aimed at Paddy. "I'm going to get a medal for killing the rebels and traitors that attacked my squad."

Helen's aim is like a roulette wheel. The barrel spins around in random directions. What she will hit, nobody knows. The weight of the weapon wears on her arms. Her vision is blurry from crying. The pain in her body is electric. She puts all her strength into it. The trigger is harder to pull than she had hoped. Her heart pumps like a steam engine's pistons. A surge of blood races through her and finds its way to her trigger finger. The shot rings out, reverberating in the hills.

The sergeant falls on his back, stunned by the bullet that just raced past his head. Paddy, confused, aims his gun at everything that moves. A frightened Wainwright takes a rushed shot at the Irishman and misses. Time hangs suspended. Everything moves at a preternatural slow and silent speed. Paddy turns his aim at Wainwright. A bullet explodes from the gun barrel, planting itself in the Englishman's gut. In the same moment, the sergeant lunges for Helen. Killing her with his weapon won't satisfy him. He needs to choke the life out of her with his bare hands.

Helen fumbles with the pistol, trying to get the chamber to advance. She looks up and sees the florid face of evil hurtling toward her. Before the sergeant can get a hand on her, Paddy drops his rifle, pulls out his service revolver, and fires a single shot. He hits his target in the back of the head. The sergeant drops like a bag of wet cement.

Time snaps back to reality. Helen can hear the birds' wings flapping in disgust at human behavior.

"I'm Eamon fucking Dougherty!"

No longer a paddy under the army's yoke, Dougherty takes stock of his actions. His chest aches, he needs air. He just shot his sergeant. Eamon fucking Dougherty has just become a fucking outlaw. *Now run.*

Dougherty abandons his British military life. He tears his uniform off down to his modesty and keeps the boots. Without giving Helen another look, he runs off into the woods.

The sergeant lies face down, blood circling his head. Nothing looks peaceful about him. He takes his anger to the afterlife etched on his face.

Helen gathers her wits and looks around. The smell of expended gunpowder burns her nose. On her hands and knees, she crawls to where Stephens lies. The young man who had the nerve to stand up to a bully and fight for an Irish woman deserves a hero's farewell kiss.

She wipes the blood from his face. An angel's face, really a baby's face. The soldier must be barely eighteen. Now he'll go home like dead meat on a butcher's tray. Helen runs her finger along his name, embroidered on his uniform over his heart.

"Stephens."

He's beautiful. Helen closes his eyes and puts her lips on his forehead. She wonders if this is his first kiss. For sure it's his last. He should have had a lot of kisses. A tear falls from her face and lands on his mouth. She looks up at Danny, still pinned to the tree. He stares at her. This is the wound that cuts him the deepest: watching his best girl give a hero's kiss to someone else. He kicks wildly at the air, but the leather belt drives itself deep into his throat.

Helen hears a moan from an Englishman. She picks up the gun and walks over to the source.

"The sergeant?" Wainwright asks meekly.

"Dead," Helen replies.

"Neely?"

"Must be the one that ran off. Coward." Helen gives no hint of what is spinning in her mind.

"Stephens?"

"Your sergeant shot him." Helen stands over her assailant.

"Dougherty, dead too?" He starts to cry. He is willing to forgive getting shot if he survives this moment.

"No, you missed. He's gone." Helen can't offer a grin but she's glad he ran off.

"Damn…. My kit, it's over there. I think I can make it with some help." Wainwright regains his English sense of importance. He struggles to sit up. The pain is searing hot. Blood spills from his stomach.

"You won't need it." Helen feels the gun heavy in her hand.

"What do you mean? It has bandages and peroxide and some morphine. Maybe your friend is a chemist or a doctor?"

Helen points the gun at the soldier. The experience of one shot taught her to get closer to the target.

"Show a little mercy. I'm just a soldier following orders." Wainwright slides on his backside away from Helen. Blood drains down his side, and his left leg is numb.

"Mercy?" Helen spits. "Where was your mercy?"

"I'm a soldier. There was an order given by my sergeant. What was I to do?" Wainwright's English sense of importance vanishes. He searches for humility.

"That boy over there knew what to do." Helen nods to her fallen hero.

Then the horrible sound of the trigger, cocked and ready.

"Please…" Wainwright continues to slide along the grass until he's blocked by the boat. He holds his arms out, pleading for everything he's worth.

"I'll give you a chance. Tell me what I want to hear." Helen gets closer, offering an ounce of hope. The pistol's barrel gets steadier. The pain in her body turns to pure energy. The gun feels light, the handle fits in her hands, the trigger soft and supple. A shudder runs up her spine. Satan whispers in her ear like a rush of wind, "Give him to me."

"What you want to hear?" The soldier searches the sky for an answer hidden behind a cloud. "I don't know what you want."

"Wrong answer. I'll give you another chance." Helen makes sure she won't miss. The distance is close. She feels steady and serene. "Now, tell me what I want to hear."

Helen holds the gun firm. She is beginning to like the way it feels in her hand.

"Fuck all. I don't know what you want." Wainwright's eyes dart around, searching for a clue.

"You know, I like your man's rule. No talking." Helen's grip on the pistol tightens. Her finger applies gentle pressure on the trigger.

"What rule? What do you want me to say?" Wainwright cries like a child, still unable to fathom what he had done wrong.

"Suddenly you're not much on taking orders. I said—no talking." Helen's focus is like a predator's. The Devil whispers: "Do it."

Helen pulls the trigger, the hammer falls, and the bullet flies. Wainwright's final moment is frozen on his face. The bullet hits him in the middle of his forehead. It leaves a clean hole, his face undisturbed except for the wide-eyed look, the same look cattle have as the hammer falls. The back of his skull splashes across the rowboat. She fires the remaining rounds into the man who raped her.

The gun is Satan's midwife. Helen falls to her knees, covered in blood. She screams like a woman in labor. The energy inside her explodes into pain. At that moment Helen feels her childhood slip away and something else born. She becomes a woman forged by violence's hot steel and not a poet's tender verse.

Easy enough to find a knife among the number of dead soldiers. Helen cuts Danny loose. There are no words to be said. Time will harvest what has been sown today.

"We have to go. Fast, Danny, we have to go as fast as we can." Helen helps him to his feet.

2: July, 1916: Wedding Day

This wasn't her dream, not exactly, not this, not here. She doesn't even know where *here* is. They are somewhere deep in the country at an old church. It looks abandoned, but it still has a priest. The bishop may have closed this church and forgot to mention the fact to Father John.

The Tinkers took them to this church because it is all but forgotten. Most of the congregation has left for America or lie buried in the yard under weather-worn headstones. The church stone walls are crumbling and consumed by overgrowth. Weeds break up the mortar. There's only one window and its wooden shutter hangs off its hinges. The slate roof has fallen to time and vandalism. Only the cross over the entrance would let anyone know this is a holy place, not just the ruin of a bygone era. Father John looks as old as the stones that built the church. He moves slowly and doesn't waste any effort. He races the sun from one side of the altar to the other. The old priest did a good job setting up the chapel. There are some stubby candles, and a few honeysuckles and gladiolas give the decay a fresh smell. Helen looks everything over with a sense of sadness. None of the people she loves most will be here. Danny of course is here, sitting silent on a stone bench, like a man awaiting the gallows.

"What about what the old woman said? Maybe that's the best thing to do." Helen doesn't mean it, but she makes the offer.

"No. We've been through that." Danny knows there aren't any simple answers.

"You know, I can always join the convent."

"Enough of that talk. You know where you'd end up." Danny stands up, angry at the suggestion. "Working in the fucking laundry till you're dead."

Father John hobbles over to Helen and Danny and gestures toward the altar.

Danny has made a wreath of wildflowers and placed it on Helen's head. The old Tinker woman gave Helen a pretty white veil that offsets her wedding dress, which is the same dress she was wearing when everything happened.

Father John mumbles his way through the service between racking coughing fits. His brogue mixed with Latin is indecipherable. His baritone voice resonates solemnly, and the stone walls echo in agreement. The wind finds its way through the cracks and crevices. Ghosts of past sacraments wake. Ignorance, famine, pestilence, Cromwell—Helen can feel the weight of their presence. Danny trembles. Angels and demons gaze down from the heavens through the fallen church roof. The odds are shown, bets placed, favorites made: let fortune play.

"The ring?" Father John flashes a broad, yellow-toothed smile. It's been a long time since he performed a wedding or any kind of sacrament.

Danny looks at Helen with shame. Helen looks away, trying to save him the torment. She holds her hand out, now looking to the red sky, wondering what cruel trick the stars are playing on her. Danny gropes around in his pockets. He finds it. Its light weight and coarse texture are embarrassing. The priest blessed it, but it doesn't seem very holy. Danny needs two hands to tie the piece of twine around Helen's wedding finger.

"You may kiss the bride." Father John runs out of breath.

Helen pulls the veil off her face and looks at Danny. She still loves him, but something is different. The wedding is a charade, a performance for the rest of the world. It just means fewer questions and less lying. This isn't the fairytale wedding little girls hold in their dreams. This is a soft, gentle nightmare playing out in the evening light.

"You may kiss the bride."

Helen and Danny clasp hands. The earth stops spinning for a moment. Hope, love, dreams, freedom, flow between their hands like an electrical current. But a kiss? Not yet. They both feel awkward. They've never kissed before. Now, under the heavens, here under the approval of God the Father, with all the hope that the future can offer as a wedding gift, the time doesn't seem right.

3: August, 1916: Tinker Camp, Ballybofey, Ireland

"I'm going in with you." Helen runs after Danny.

"Aoife said it is a meeting just for the men."

Helen doesn't like things she can't control. With hands on hips, she circles Danny like a boxer searching for a soft spot.

"Look, let me hear what the man from Dublin has to say. I promise I will repeat every word."

"And I'm going to want to know just how he said it." Helen pokes Danny in the chest.

"I swear to God and all the saints and martyrs." Danny crosses himself.

Helen doesn't like it. She watches Danny disappear into the caravan.

Aoife, an ancient Tinker woman, comes out of the caravan with a whiskey in hand.

"Come to the fire." Aoife puts a bony arm around Helen to console her. "Let the men talk. The cards are being shown. I'm afraid your man was dealt a shite hand."

"What does that mean?" Helen throws the old woman's arm off.

"It means the IRB man is going to pay for your ticket to America. Your man just has to do something for him," Aoife snaps.

"The IRB?" Helen knows nothing good will come from that. "And if he refuses?"

"I guess they leave his dead body at the front door of the police barracks."

4: August, 1916: Danny meets the IRB

The summer's sun rests on the River Finn. It's quiet, the way the country is supposed to be. There's a war a continent away, but out here, in the country, the birds sing and children play. The air is filled with smoke from campfires and roasted game. Music plays and poteen pours. It's just another night in Tinker heaven. Danny was told to show up at the old Tinker woman's caravan. Her advice is simple: keep your gob shut and let the chips land around you.

Dark clouds roll in with a rumble. In the distance, above the mountains, a cluster of lightning flashes. Seconds later, the thunder sounds. Danny imagines demons and angels squaring off in the heavens. Armor-clad angels using broad swords to strike righteousness into the hideous hearts of demons. Little does he realize they are rolling dice and his soul is in the winner's pot.

Danny knocks on the caravan door and is let in. He finds two men and the old lady waiting for him at the table. The oil lamp's blackened glass flute glows, revealing nothing about the interior.

"There's some gentlemen from Dublin here to see you." Aoife, the old Tinker woman, makes the introductions. At arm's length, she lights her long clay pipe and puffs with quiet confidence. "They want to help."

Danny tries to figure out what these two men would want with him.

They sit in silence for an uncomfortable period. Danny rocks in his seat, anxious and curious. The two men sit like stone. The oil lamp hangs from the ceiling. It creates deep, soulless shadows under their eyes. One of them lights a cigarette and his face glows for a moment. It's an older man, with a goatee and round wire glasses. Danny thought the man could pass for a schoolmaster.

"Whiskey?" The older man offers. There's a bottle beside some glasses on the table.

"No, thank you." Danny's not drinking until he has something to celebrate. He hasn't had a drink since…

"Mind if we have a glass?" The older man pours from the bottle into two glasses.

Again the silence commands attention.

Then it's finally broken.

"Do you know this man?" The older man nods toward the fellow next to him.

Danny shakes his head no, not really sure of his answer.

"Does the name Eamon Dougherty mean anything to you?"

Danny racks his brain, thinking of school friends, people in town. Nothing comes to mind.

"Eamon Dougherty. Are you sure?"

The younger man lifts his cap and leans into the lamp light. His face takes form in the soft light. It takes a moment, but Danny begins to understand.

"I thought you might know each other." The older man takes a large drag off his smoke and throws the drink down as if his life depends on it.

"This is where I let the men talk." Aoife pours herself a glass of the Irish and closes the door behind her.

The older man lets her go without notice. He pours another drink for himself. He gives Danny a look as if it's Judgment Day.

"On behalf of the Irish Republican Brotherhood, the Irish Volunteers, and free Irishmen everywhere, we appreciate the crimes you suffered at the hands of the British." The older man looks over at Dougherty, then back to Danny. "The result of the action that took place. We are happy to add Mr. Dougherty to our ranks. He found his patriotism when it counted the most. And we feel your missus, as result of her ... well ... we see her as a combatant. Up the Republic."

"Up the Republic." Dougherty joins the IRB man in the toast and holds his glass up high.

Danny sits in silence. He isn't sure what this means.

"If it wasn't for Mr. Dougherty, I don't think we would be sitting here today. Do you?" It's a rhetorical question from the IRB man.

Danny doesn't say anything. He can't disagree. At the same time, this is the same fucking bastard that pinned him to that tree.

"I know you're a young country boy. You probably never held a gun before. You have no training as a soldier. But you did what you had to do, as a man and a free Irishman." The IRB man tips his hat. "Don't let it prey on you. It's understandable to have—high emotions. Personally, I would have cut their cocks off and stuffed them in their dead mouths."

Danny tries to understand what the IRB man is getting to.

"Now as far as the British are concerned, you and the missus, as well as Mr. Dougherty, are to be hanged as soon as possible. As far as they're concerned, you're ghosts walking. They're not going to let things out of control in the countryside. Two rebel lovebirds and a traitorous soldier hanged for sedition. Makes a good headline. So I'd like to help you and your woman leave Ireland. Would that be fine with you?"

The dice are rolling all around Danny.

"Mr. Dougherty is going abroad himself, at least for a while. He's going to learn a new language, German, maybe—we'll see. Do you like fishing?" The older man laughs. "You seem like a good young man. Taking care of his woman, fighting the Brits. You're a smart lad, worked for a newspaper. Right. The Republic is going to need lads like you."

Danny nods.

"You have a sense of fairnesss, don't you?" The IRB man pushes Danny toward an answer.

"I hope so."

"Ah, he's a good Irish Catholic lad." The IRB man nudges Dougherty with a sharp elbow. "So, with that said, do you think you could do Mr. Dougherty, here, and the IRB, a small favor?"

Danny thinks, this is what I've heard about. The way the IRB entices young men into their ranks. On the other hand, the Brits aren't doing much to win Irish hearts.

"How small?" Danny can feel a trickle of cold sweat run down his spine.

"We need someone to drop off a package in a pub in Derry. If you can do that, there's two hundred in American dollars and a place for you and the missus on a trawler leaving Buncrana." The IRB man lays his cards on the table. "That should help start a new life over there."

"What's in the package?" A fool's question.

"Let's just say it's a debt payment." The IRB man grins.

5: September, 1916: Derry, Ulster

At the appointed time, Danny makes his way to the bridge over the River Foyle. He can hear the clock strike eleven from the Londonderry Guildhall's clock tower. There is a man in the center of the bridge and not another soul around. He wears a long trench coat, a wool cap down over his eyes, and the marking red scarf around his neck. At his feet is a leather satchel with a shamrock embossed on the side.

"It's a good night for fishing." Danny feels foolish saying it, but that's the greeting he is supposed to deliver.

"Not for the fish." A passionless reply comes from under the wool cap.

"Do you have a package for me?" Danny hopes he doesn't.

"At my feet." The man with the red scarf turns to Danny. "Remember, have one pint and leave. You want to look like you're waiting for a friend. There will be a car waiting for you down by the quays."

Danny nods like a child trying his best.

The man with the red scarf disappears across the bridge. Danny picks up the satchel, heavy for its size, and walks the other way. He rehearsed the route the night before so he wouldn't get lost in the warren of medieval streets leading to the Red Branch Pub. He's told it's after closing but the pub will be still crowded with a private party, and not to worry, it's the right kind of people. There is an operative there who needs the cash for bribes. The IRB needs a fresh face in the district to make the transfer. Danny isn't famous in Derry yet, so he is ideal for this operation.

Music and loud voices break up an otherwise quiet night. The lights are mostly out in the neighborhood except for the Red Branch. Above the front door is a shield with a painted red fist holding a sword, with a crimson branch underneath.

The pub is crowded. Pints are being tossed back as if it's a competition. There's a dance band playing popular songs. Danny walks in unnoticed. He goes straight to the coat rack by the front door. He hangs the satchel on a hook, then covers it with his coat. Something is strange about the crowd, but Danny shrugs it off. He puts his head down to avoid eye contact and goes straight to the bar. He is supposed to order a Guinness. They didn't say he had to drink it. Maybe he'll have a pint when he gets to America with Helen. Then they'll celebrate.

"Guinness." Danny raises his hand to get the barkeep's attention.

"Who the fuck are you?" One look at Danny, and the barkeep knows an outsider when he sees one.

Danny is surprised by the greeting. He looks around to see if anyone else saw the indignity he just suffered. Then the penny drops. Rifles by the door, gun belts hung on the backs of chairs. Shite, gun belts on hips. The pub is open to entertain the troops. It's one khaki-clad soldier after another, mixed with some civilians and local trollops. Danny wears the scent of someone not from Derry. Fuck, better call it Londonderry. He turns back to the bartender.

"I'm looking for someone. I think I made a mistake." Danny apologizes and walks toward the door, trying not to run. He grabs his coat and gives the satchel one last look. He's confused. Does he run back to his handlers with the payroll or …?

Somewhere beyond the clouds the demons are laughing. Danny realizes where he fits into tonight's game of chance. Are the angels amused? He's nothing more than a chess piece being sacrificed for a bigger play.

Danny couldn't have been in the pub more than four minutes and can't keep his feet from running. He feels himself flying across curbs and over cobblestones down an empty street. Then it hits. A flash followed by the roar of thunder. He tries not to look back like Lot's wife. The Red Branch's windows shatter. Chaos breaks out. Smoke and flaming debris fill the street. Survivors stagger out beyond the curb in shock. Danny is knocked down and gets covered in grime. His ears ring like one endless church gong.

A well-dressed woman falters in front of him. She's a bit plump and still breathing. Danny can tell from her clothes she is a member of the class above, maybe an officer's wife. She has one white glove on, and one off.

It's the missing glove hand that attracts his eye. A wedding band with a big diamond reflects the carnage and flames surrounding them.

Mixed with the din, a voice from beyond the clouds leans into Danny's ear and says two simple words: "Take it."

Another voice, more mortal in origin, implores, "Help me."

Danny doesn't know what to do. His ears ring and his head pounds like a riveter's hammer.

Danny helps the woman sit up. She is too large for his small frame to move far. He tries to make her comfortable. He uses the hem of her torn dress to wrap a cut above her elbow. Next, he takes his coat off and places it under the woman's head. She has some scrapes above her eyes. Danny guesses her white hair makes her someone's Granny. Then she shatters the gentle moment within a savage one.

"Those goddam Fenians should be hanged," she shrieks to anyone within earshot. "Don't you think, dear. You must be one of the good ones."

"I like to think so." Danny holds the woman by the hand, comforting her pain.

"Where's my son?" the plump woman asks. She looks straight into Danny's soul. "Why?"

Her hand is in Danny's. Her tight grip gives way.

"I don't know." He knows full well why.

Everything has a price. Danny exacts his price as he slides his hand across the old woman's. Her lavish wedding ring is the fee procured. Danny gets up and snatches his coat back from under the woman. She falls backward unceremoniously.

Through the ringing in his ears, the voice in his brain screams.

"Run."

6: September, 1916: Leaving Ireland

"Start warming the engines. We leave within the hour." The trawler's captain starts barking orders.

"Danny isn't here," Helen worries.

"Tide waits for no man, and neither do I." The captain looks at his watch and walks down the old wooden pier. He's not running the risk of being caught in the low tide.

Helen sees a man, bound and gagged, escorted up the gangway by a couple of dicey characters. His eyes are blood red from crying.

"Looks like we have an extra passenger," the captain says.

It's a trawler by class and a floating miracle by maritime standards, a bucket of rusted bolts and a steam engine that dates back to the beginning of its kind. By contract and lack of another floating vessel, this might be considered the IRB's flagship. It's wartime. The North Atlantic respects no boundaries; the trawler is supplied with flags of all the combatants as well as the United States and Mexico. The trawler's name, Neptune's Folly, offers no national preference. It hopes to slide between the waves, storms, and icebergs unnoticed. The ship's mission is to bring guns and cash from America and maybe catch some fish for appearances.

Helen runs over to the IRB commander. His trench coat, wide-brimmed hat, and long rifle slung over his shoulder make him look more like a gangster than commander of a shadow army. There is no news from Derry. Out here on this isolated peninsula, there's no electricity, no telegraphs, no telephones. The tide will be racing before dawn, and the trawler needs to be with it. If the mission went as planned, Danny should have been here by now.

"Here, take this." The commander hands Helen a pistol. "It's a long trip. The crew can get… you know… you may have to…"

Helen understands and takes it.

"This should help get you started in America." The IRB commander peels off ten crisp U.S. ten-dollar bills.

"What's this?" Helen holds the money in her hand. "It's supposed to be two hundred dollars."

"For two people. I only see one."

"Where is he?" Helen demands, with nothing to back up her demand other than her attitude.

"He's either been caught, or he's dead. The odds were against him."

The words hit hard. Danny—caught, dead—impossible.

The trawler's engine belches smoke. Topside, the crew goes about the business of casting off. Supplies, packages, contraband, the last-minute needs for a three-week trip across the North Atlantic are loaded onto the deck. The night sky yields to sunrise's violence. Seagulls fly screaming at the sun's intrusion. The whistle blows.

There's an argument from below decks, loud enough to be heard above the diesel engine.

"I don't care. He'll want to eat, then we'll have to give him water. Fuck, then he's going to want to take a shit. Do it now, and we'll deal with him when we're in open water. The fish are always hungry."

"I still haven't heard what I want to hear," an angry voice roars.

"He's never going to say it. Just do it." Anger from another voice answers.

"Time to go," the captain shouts from the deck.

"He needs more time. Please." Helen is frantic. She darts around the pier searching for someone to understand. "I can't leave without him."

"Sorry, Miss. You're either staying here alone or coming with us. I don't care which," the captain shouts.

"Lights coming our way." A shout comes from the crow's nest.

Men come flying out of the ship's belly, guns drawn, bolted for action.

Helen runs down to the end of the pier, her hair flying in the wind. Her heart pounds. She sees the car stop. Four men get out. Danny is one of them.

"Stand down." Someone barks orders in the dark.

The IRB commander walks up and taps Helen on the shoulder.

"Here." He peels ten crisp bills off a stack. Then, in an uncharacteristic gesture for a hardened soldier, he adds, "Here. I know." His eyes glance down at Helen's stomach.

"Some of the women from the Volunteers put together a bag of clothes for you. There might even be a coat for your man. You're going to need every stitch you can wear once you're out on the ocean." He hands Helen a tightly packed duffel bag. He takes a few steps away before a final thought comes to his mind. "You know this all is for nothing if we can't take care of each other. I may be a soldier, and I may have done some things, but…"

Helen looks at him, astonished. She takes the dollar bills and crushes them in her hand.

"Thank you." Emotions overtake her from every direction.

"Danny!" Helen rushes toward her man and holds him tight. "What happened? Where have you been?"

"What?" Danny holds Helen at arm's length. "I can't hear you."

"I said, Danny. . ." Helen, confused, pulls him back.

"There was a loud noise. It hurt my ears—my head is roaring. I'll be all right."

A sound like a clap of thunder: a muzzle flash lights up the windows in the trawler's wheelhouse. The sharp sound feels like a smack to the back of Helen's head. Danny leaps half out of his skin.

"Come on then, get on," the captain shouts. The lines are tossed and the trawler drifts away from the pier to the engine's rhythm.

7: September, 1916: North Atlantic

It's dark in their cabin. It's more like a storage closet with bunks. The supplies stacked in the corner confirm that notion. Gray starlight creeps through the portal like a spotlight demanding an actor.

"I see they gave us the honeymoon quarters," Danny says from the top bunk. "Excellent service. Top people."

"Better than we would get at Dublin Castle," Helen jokes. "Service is terrible at the castle. But I hear the executions are well done. Always on time."

"Maybe, but the mattress here feels like corporal punishment," Danny says. "And the meals are a slow form of execution."

"I wish this fucking thing would stop moving for one moment." Helen braces herself against the bunk frame. The ship's constant vibration makes her sick, the smell of bilge water makes her sick, fumes make her sick, food makes her sick, and what stirs inside her makes her sick.

Danny slides off his bunk and sits beside Helen. With one hand he rubs her back, and with the other, he holds her long hair.

"I need another arm to hold a bucket." Danny tries to put on a brave face.

"You need to shut up and make this thing stop." It's too late.

"Oh, Jesus," Helen prays. Like a storm at low tide, everything in her stomach spills to the cabin's floor.

"Agh, that smells awful. Let me get something to clean up with." Danny dances around the spillage. "I think I'm getting sick."

Danny makes a quick exit. The air in the hallway below deck isn't much better. He finds his way down to the engine room and borrows a stack of rags and a bucket of sawdust. The rags were washed but still reek of oil. He hopes that smell doesn't stir things up again.

Walking back to the cabin, Danny puts his hand in his pocket. It's still there, wrapped in a beautifully embroidered handkerchief.

Danny opens the cabin door and the vapors of hell escape. He grabs a deep breath and goes in.

"It'll be better once I clean up this mess." Danny is on hands and knees, more out of surrender than cleaning efficiency.

"I need a priest for an exorcism. I must be empty, nothing has come out in a while." Helen's voice is weak.

"You got every drop of the devil out of you." Danny continues to slop up the swill that runs away with each roll of the boat. He covers the area with sawdust to dry up what couldn't be ragged up.

Helen is sitting up in her bunk, slowly drinking water.

"You must be feeling better. There's a dance later, will you be up for it? I'm sure you'll be the prettiest girl at the ball," Danny says.

"Finally I get the attention I've always craved." Danny has made Helen smile.

"You are feeling better. Good." Danny strokes Helen's hair. He looks at her in silence for a long time. For a prolific poet, he's at a loss for words, at least good ones.

"I know there is a crew of men running around the ship, but this is the first time we've been really alone. No Tinker kids in our business. It's not the best way, I know. I wish it could be more romantic or at least not roll back and forth so much." Danny steadies himself against the bunk frame. "I don't know what lies ahead. With our luck, a sea monster will take a bite out of this rust bucket and spit it out."

"Our luck to run into a picky beast." Helen laughs, and it hurts her strained abdomen muscles.

Danny moves up to his knees and reaches into his pocket.

He has no words for what he has to show her. Danny unfolds the handkerchief. He moves his hand around, trying to find enough light.

"Oh Sweet Jesus. It's brilliant." Helen grabs the diamond-studded gold ring from Danny, not willing to wait for ceremony.

"Danny, this must have cost a king's ransom. How did you pay for it?" Her excitement is undone by logic. "What did you do? You were with the IRB men." The ring is already on her hand. Helen extends her arm and looks at the way the gold catches the starlight. "I should throw this into the ocean. All we need is a robbery charge to go with sedition and murder. But... damn it, Danny, it's beautiful."

Danny pulls Helen close. He rubs his cheek on her head, enjoying the softness of her hair.

"Don't worry. There is a shop in Derry owned by a man—sympathetic to the Republic. He gave me quite a deal."

"Where is this shop?"

"I was in Derry so fast, I don't remember the name of the shop or street."

Helen examines the ring in the dim light. She puts it back on her finger and mimes showing it off to friends.

"You're a liar," she says.

"What? It's true."

"If you love me, promise me you will never tell me the truth about the ring." Helen smacks him on the head.

"I told you—I got a bargain!"

"Shite, Danny. You're a terrible liar and worse actor." Helen settles into her bunk. "Let's not talk of it again. I'm sure it's a good story, but a girl needs to have some illusions. It's beautiful, and I love you. Now bring me a bucket, I'm going to throw up."

Danny complies like a gentleman. He positions the bucket close to her mouth. He kisses the top of her head and pulls the blanket up to her shoulders. Quietly, he takes the blanket off his bunk and covers her. Helen falls asleep without resistance.

Danny climbs into his bunk. He uses the clothes from the duffel bag to make a nest for himself. His eyes are heavy. After everything they've been through, it seems peaceful here. He is going to have to reconcile some things. The moral ledger is in the red. He feels the world owes him something. But tonight he sleeps comfortably, knowing his wife is happy and safe, at least for tonight. They went to sleep many nights when they couldn't say that. They're safe at sea as long as God desires. Danny rolls over with the expectation of a good night's sleep.

The first splash hits the bucket, followed by a rhythmic volley.

****

Danny steps out on the trawler's deck. It's cold, but the air is clean. Helen is asleep down below. It's best for her to sleep when she can. This trip is miserable. He can only imagine what she's going through. He'll have to get her up on deck to get some fresh air. The endless chug of the engine is starting to drive him mad.

He found it by accident, but feels a bit guilty going through what little Helen owns. He took it. At first, he didn't know what to do with it. Now it's in his pocket. The crewmen pass by, too busy to notice Danny. He's more in the way. Just as well. Danny thinks the captain would be none too thrilled to find out what was in his pocket. He's just guessing, trying to justify his thoughts.

That night in Derry haunts his dreams. For what? So Helen can puke in the bowels of this garbage scow? There's another nightmare that pokes him at night. It likes to appear just as he's falling asleep. It's Helen, holding the soldier's pistol. The chilling part is her serene expression, then the sound the bullet makes as it rips through the atmosphere. There's enough spilled blood surrounding them. Fuck, we're just two country kids, we should be going to a Ceilidh dance.

Danny feels it in his pocket, cold and hard. Even if it was needed, Danny wouldn't know what to do with it. Damn, Helen would. That does it. That makes the choice for him.

Danny looks at his hands. Scrub them all he wants, they're not coming clean, not after Derry. He pulls it out of his pocket. Danny looks down at the ocean steaming past at five knots. He can't think about it anymore. This has to end somewhere. He lets the revolver fall to the depths.

8: October, 1916: Baltimore

Everyone on the trawler said the weather was good in the North Atlantic for this time of year, but you couldn't prove it by talking to Helen. She's exhausted, damp, hungry, and feels like shit. Her stomach sloshed counter to the trawler's rolling among the waves. She grew tired of watching the captain and crew go from nervous to petrified every time a shadow was spotted on the endless gray horizon. English destroyers, German U-boats, icebergs, storms, there was no quarter, no forgiveness at sea for the weak.

They made it. It took three weeks, but it felt like years. The Chesapeake Bay is like an oversized lake compared to the unruly North Atlantic. Calm water, land on two sides. The wind has bit less bite than the open ocean. Helen's stomach has gotten bigger despite the miserable meals and the endless sea sickness. She looks over at Danny still sleeping, curled up in a fetal position. There is a lot to complain about, but Danny isn't one of them. He's been blindly loyal as no soldier or dog could ever be. But then so little has been asked of him since they've been on this wretched garbage scow. All there is to do is sleep, eat, and throw up.

Here they are, cruising through a busy harbor blending in with the other working boats. Tugs, skipjacks, skiffs, and barges float past the old fort and army hospital. Baltimore was the perfect destination. With its large Irish immigrant population, Helen and Danny can slip into oblivion easy enough, but the IRB was more concerned with a safe harbor, helpful natives, bribable officials and cases of Enfield rifles. Helen's having family in the city was a lucky accident.

There's a knock on the cabin door.

"Helen?" The captain knocks again. "We're almost ready to go ashore. I need you to do something."

The cabin door opens part way. Helen mostly trusts the captain; at least he hasn't done anything untrustworthy.

"What?"

"I have paperwork for you and your man. But you'll have to pass yourself off as a crewman." The captain looks down at the bump in Helen's belly, then up to her long hair. "I guess we need to make you a fat man."

Helen offers a small smile as she grasps the situation. She looks over at her man, thin as a blade of grass, starting to wake up.

"I might need some pants." Helen shakes her head.

The trawler rafts next to Miss Fortune, a tug tied up alongside Henderson's Wharf. Dock space is at a premium, and there are business matters to attend. The captain looks for his contact while his crew works with the tug's crew. The contact should be easy enough to find. If it's like Ireland, Hasidim are a rare breed. The wharf is busy with foot traffic and hand trollies shoving goods bound to keep England and France from starving. Even though the captain is an experienced hand, it still takes him a bit of getting used to going from the solitary humdrum of life at sea to the shock of returning to the chaotic world on shore. And rumor has it Baltimore is still suffering from the Spanish Flu.

Down the wharf the Customs Inspection Officer walks alongside a small man dressed in pure black. His shoes are well worn and lack any attempt of a shine. The hem of his coat is ragged and frayed. His prized possession may well be the black fur wide-brimmed shtreimel on his head. Below the shtreimel the distinctive long curls and gray beard frame the face of a Hasidic scholar. They approach Miss Fortune's captain for a brief discussion.

The trawler's captain observes his contact. Coming down the wharf are a couple of coppers. His gut tightens. He looks over on the deck of the tug. A stack of crates meant for his boat's belly sit exposed. Who knows what spies are lurking in the crowd? The Crown has eyes everywhere. Is the Jew going to trade us for some coin, or is it business as usual? The coppers walk up to the Customs Officer with a tip of the hat. The captain inches up on the rigging trying in vain to read lips. He sees a lot of smiles and handshakes. So far, so good. The coppers fuck off and continue down the wharf. There it is, in the wink of an eye, two envelopes exchange hands. The good Hasid gifts the Customs Officer and tugboat captain an acceptable value for their favors.

"Let's go." The captain calls down to Helen and Danny.

Helen waddles through the companion way with Danny providing emotional and physical support.

"Up she goes." Danny puts his shoulder to his wife's rump and shoves her up to the deck.

Helen had grown used to the fresh ocean wind that made breathing free and easy. Now tied up in port, there's no wind. She feels as if she's suffocating. Below-decks reek of diesel, bilge water, and salt stained crewman. On deck the air is ugly: smoke billows out of Sparrow Point factories and coal dust wafts across from Curtis Bay. Black diesel clouds follow the ships and tugs like dark ghosts. The sun hangs low in the sky, a dim ball of gray light.

Helen turns to the captain for his inspection. He adjusts her pea coat and pulls her cap closer to her eyes.

"This isn't for that man in uniform with his shiny badge. He's paid well enough to forget what he sees. It's the unseen eyes from unknown places I worry about." The captain gives Helen a wishful look and shakes Danny's hand. "Keep up the act till the Jew tells you it's safe. Good luck to you both."

The Captain shows Helen and Danny the way across the planks going from trawler to tug to shore.

The crew men line up with their papers in hand to be stamped by the Customs Officer. A scruffier lot couldn't be found.

"OO-OO-AH-AH. Smells like a boatload the monkeys climbing off the boat— eh. I'm sorry—meant a boatload of mickeys." The Customs Officer laughs at his own joke. His humor doesn't go far.

"Not much luck with the fish—eh." Another joke gone flat.

"Engine trouble, mate. We're in for some work." The captain doesn't like the talkative Customs Officer. That's how things can go wrong, too much talking.

Helen and Danny take their place in the line. Passports and seaman papers look impressive enough, but an expert eye would see them as the forgeries they are. That's what the Customs Officer is paid to do. Not look for details.

"And who do we have here?" The Customs Officer notices Helen's soft hands. "What do you do on board?"

Helen gives him a blank look. The Customs Officer pulls out a cigar from his breast pocket. With the flick of a lighter he gets it billowing smoke like a tug's exhaust. He blows a puff of smoke in Helen's face.

"On board, your job? What is your task on the boat? Sailor?" The Customs Officer smiles knowing he's hitting a raw nerve.

Helen looks around, first at the Hasid, then at the captain. Her mouth flops around but words are failing.

"Cook's mate. This is the cook and cook's mate." The captain intervenes. He wants to get his passengers off and be on his way. There's a shipment full of guns and contraband that needs loading. He readies the switchblade in his pocket in case this Customs Officer trades sides.

"The lad can't speak for himself?" The Customs Officer keeps pushing.

"Excuse me, captain. My name is Rabbi Edelman. I'm your agent in America." The man in black breaks in. His thick Yiddish accent is filled with inflections, but his English is spot on. "Let me talk to the man in charge here."

The Hasid turns and looks up at the Customs Officer.

"Our business here is done. But I still need to come to your office for some signatures and stamps. In the meantime, I promised my good friend, Father O'Malley over at St. Mary's, you may know him, I'd bring these to crewmen to their relatives for a visit. So if you don't mind we will be off. Good day. Captain—Officer."

Before the Customs Officer can react, Edelman grabs Helen and Danny by the arm and whisks them up Ann Street in the warehouse shadows. He leads them across Thames Street toward their final destination. It's the end of the IRB's long arm. Despite the stubborn clinging of the Spanish Flu, Fells Point is alive with war fever. At least, cash fever. The docks are stacked with goods ready to go to Europe. Mountains of goods are being fed into the bellies of the great freighters. Patriotic gibberish is on everyone's tongue. Talk of U-boat torpedoes and British destroyers confiscating goods are on the lips from the lowest stevedore to the captains of transatlantic trade.

The energy of the place makes Danny's heart race. Helen is overwhelmed by the noise and pace. Danny sees a city that doesn't give a shite about kings and Kaisers. They're walking around in a different world. No risk of rebellion, no soldiers spoiling the craic, no spies, martyrs or traitors on every corner. Only a few boarded shops bearing signs saying Plague Is Over Re-Opening Soon. Helen wonders how they're going to fit into this strange place.

"Don't worry. It will get better with time." Edelman senses Helen's discomfort. His raspy voice has an empathic quality. "Everyone here is from somewhere else. Everyone has a past no one wants to talk about. Keep your secrets to yourself and start over."

Edelman walks with bent over shoulders and ancient knees. He aches as he labors over the cobblestones. Helen and Danny have their own problems walking. Weeks on a rolling trawler make navigating on land a chore. At first they walk like a comic vaudeville duo leaning on each other as they stumble along. That appearance devolves into looking like a pair of mid-morning drunks tumbling their way home. Finally Helen has to stop.

"Sweet Jesus, are we walking back to Donegal? Where is this place?" Helen is winded and sways back and forth.

"Not much further. Your friends from Ireland want me to deliver you both to the Cat's Eye Pub. It has a reputation for being friendly to your cause," Edelman assures her.

A mile out on the Patapsco River an in-bound freighter blasts its horn calling for tugboat services. The Cat's Eye Pub explodes open at the horn's call. Competing tugboat crews battle through the door, throwing punches, sweeping legs, wrestling. The tugboat industry is a dog-eat-dog business. It's a race to meet the inbound ship.

Edelman opens the door to the pub letting daylight in and rabble out. The yellowed walls are covered in cheap painted mythologies of the old sod. Gas lamps barely light up the few Gaelic Athletic Association banners and rebel slogans that hang on the walls. The bar man looks up and sees a Jew enter the establishment. He puts his bar rag down and disappears into the bar's sacristy behind closed doors. A moment later he reappears with another man behind him. Edelman gives a nod and a wink, a signal to let the men behind the bar know all is well. Even if America isn't in the war, that doesn't mean it's not involved. Spies take advantage of the split allegiances the Irish and German immigrants have. No love lost in this establishment for the English. The Easter Rebellion is still a fresh punch to the gut among the natives and the immigrants.

Danny feels both at home and a new sense of freedom. He eyes the taps at the bar and licks his lips. It's been since, well it's been since . . . then. Helen can't believe they had to cross the ocean to end up here.

Edelman leads Helen and Danny to a table where a woman waits, dressed in her worn Sunday best.

"Oh dear God . You must be Helen." The woman looks up in delight and surprise. "The last photograph I saw was you in your communion dress. I guess that was the last time I heard from your mother."

Helen is at a loss for words. Her mouth is dry as sand. She's feeling flushed and overheated. Danny sees her sweating and helps her get her coat off.

"A man shows up at my door and says my family in the old country needs my help. There's been some trouble but he doesn't say what kind." The woman looks at Helen's stomach then glares at Danny. "Well I guess it doesn't take an imagination who caused the trouble. And dear God, what about the costume?"

Danny wants to scream at the woman. She has no idea who caused the trouble. It's a nightmare he wants to put out of his mind. Helen squeezes his hand holding him in check.

"Yes, well. It's a long story. I would like to get out of these." Helen shakes off the pea coat and reveals her fisherman's attire.

"I'm Helen, of course, and this is my husband Danny." Helen smiles with the grace and sincerity of a stage actor. Then she holds up two fingers. "And it's two. Twins. Two."

"Sweet Mother Mary, the devil gave a little of himself. Twins, well that's just one more mouth to feed." Margie stokes and lights the stove that sets Danny's blood boiling. "And this is the weed of a man you hitched your hopes and dreams to?"

"Who does this judgmental…?" Danny asks himself. Helen takes his hand to calm him down, before he can utter his thought: Who does this judgmental bitch think she is?

"I'm sorry, I'm your aunt Margie. I'm related to Helen's mother—but you know that. I don't know where your uncle Frank is. He's usually very punctual." Margie is a large woman who is almost as tall as Helen even though she's sitting. "You poor thing, I can only imagine what you've been through."

Danny rolls his eyes and clenches his teeth. This woman has surely found a way to get under his skin. And she speaks like a loud native of Baltimore, not even a hint of the old country in her voice.

"Well, at least, he married you." That's as close to anything nice as Margie is going to say.

Edelman clears his throat. "Now that you are all united, my obligations are met. I still need to go to the Customs House. Remember what I said." The old rabbi puts a finger to his lips.

"All right then. Thank you Mr. Edelman. Thank your Irish friends for finding me." Margie rises from her chair. "Now then, we can take the trolley and head home."

Danny stares at the woman. Three fucking weeks at sea and she doesn't offer a man a chance for a drink. At least offer some comfort and food for the missus. She's with child—children—for godsake. This would never stand back home. We made it. We are alive. Finally something to celebrate. Is how they do things in this country? Let an old woman push her will on everyone? Danny grabs the one bag between them and helps Helen lumber to her feet. Margie ploughs a path through the daytime crowd at the bar. Helen follows in her wake, still swaying to the rhythm of the waves. Danny staggers behind, eyeing the taps at the bar pouring sweet amber ale into large glasses. He licks his lips.

9: January, 1917: The Baptism

Winter's light comes through the stained glass windows as cold as the wind that blows outside. Helen and Margie fuss over the twins while Father Xavier paces impatiently back and forth in the transept. The neighborhood hens are stirring in the pews. They're a flock of Irish women, a combination of natives and immigrants, with their ill-behaved chicks in tow. They come to witness, support, judge, and gossip. In the back of the church are two men from the Cat's Eye Pub. They stand in the shadows following up on their investments.

"It is almost twelve noon. We have a mother and Godmother, but no father and Godfather." Father Xavier's potato-shaped nose drips, an eternal fount of nasal maladies. He pulls a handkerchief from his vestment's sleeve and wipes his nose. "There is another baptism and a wedding in the church this afternoon, not to mention confessions."

"Just give him five more minutes. Danny has a flair for the dramatic." Helen pleads.

"The first time Frank shows any interest in you two—and something happens. He and Danny are up to no good, I tell you. No good." Margie rocks the borrowed baby buggy violently.

Helen sees the women in the pews and feels the burn of judging eyes. She's heard all the rumors and speculation around her and Danny's arrival. Nobody's theory is even close. Gaelic kinship isn't immune to the worst of human nature. The neighborhood gossips have created a legend where nothing is true. Helen's reputation has to be assassinated to make the story work. Trouble with two men, trouble with family, trouble with the IRB, trouble with the crown, trouble, trouble. Trouble is all anyone can imagine. After all, Helen and Danny appeared out of thin air.

Worse than the neighbors are the two men lurking in the shadows. Even if they were dressed as circus clowns, they would still look like IRB men. Are they checking on Danny? Did they have more for Danny to do? Do they own him? Where the hell is Danny?

Danny's morning started off early, following orders. He kept his mouth shut and did whatever Helen or Margie commanded. Since the twins arrived, he's been sullen. He stares at the two baby boys as if he is looking into the face of all that's evil. Beyond the pale, the two little bastards stare back with mocking glances. At some point, Frank announced he knew a tailor who could set Danny up with a suit to wear for the day. So Danny was rushed off to see the tailor. This is where details become uncertain.

Danny tosses another shot down the hatch and shuts his eyes. He doesn't realize he's alone at the bar. An empty glass and cigar smoldering in the ashtray are all that remains of his uncle-in-law Frank.

There was a time before. A time before all this happened. Danny looks at his empty shot glass. *Back in the old days when I loved the Gaelic Revival. Loved its writers and artists. Learned the new songs, the new poetry. I was going to be a great writer mentioned among the giants. Just a matter of time before the rest of the world caught up. But the war in Europe fucked everything. Ireland was fucked. I was fucked.*

Danny turns, looking for Frank to order another round. These are the first drops of alcohol Danny has had since … and it's gone straight to his head. His legs are a bit wobbly. Taking it slow may have been a better plan, but it's too late now. Danny has downed enough to make up for lost time, and the clock hands barely touch noon.

"Where did you go?" Danny stumbles around looking for Frank. "For the love of Christ."

"Hey, mate." The bartender waves at Danny getting his attention. "Your man said he had to fuck off. Said something about feeling lucky on some kind of business."

"What? He said what?" Danny tries to solve the puzzle.

"Oh, another thing, he said something about a church." The bartender isn't concerned with delivering the message in its full detail.

"Church?" Danny scratches his head. The room is spinning, and his empty stomach isn't handling four quick shots of straight whiskey. "What the fuck's at the church?"

At the church, the women's voices drone on like a Gregorian chant. They grate Helen's ears. Even the hard-of-hearing old priest can hear the muttering over his nasal slurps.

A bit late for the father to run out Never too late for a bosthoon to run off Just the sight of him. He's got the look of hunger about him What about her? Who are her people? She has the look of trouble about her Pounds for a ring on the finger but not a penny for food in the stomach or clothes for the back The babies look very small. Does anyone feed them? They got faces only a mother can love—

I SAID NO TALKING! Helen's head throbs with the words, yet she stays silent.

"Maybe there's been an accident?" The good reverend tries to manage a solution to his schedule. "Would you like to postpone? We can do it during the week."

Winter light explodes through the church doors. For a moment, the whole of the nave is illuminated as if by a photographer's flash. Everyone turns toward the light. A silhouetted figure commands the congregation's attention.

"There's only one of them." Hands on hips, Margie can guess which one is missing.

"I told you he would make an entrance." Helen smiles, sure it's Danny ready to take his place as a father.

The women in the pews don't share Helen's optimism. They see a twig of a boy pretending to be a man stumbling down the aisle. Plaster saints stare down with disinterest, but Danny can't resist giving them a salute off the bill of his cap.

"Right then. Are we ready to sancti-sanctify the little buggers?" Danny is tripping over his feet and words.

"Where's the suit? Where's Frank? Why do you smell like a distillery?" Margie has her nose inches away from Danny. "And take the cap off. Show some goddam respect."

"All fair questions, Madame." Danny's smile is as false as a three-dollar bill. "But in my defense…"

"Damn it. We will get to the bottom of this later. Right now I want my children baptized in the name of the … Lord."

Father Xavier, an experienced pastor, hangs his head, knowing the futility of intervening in family arguments.

"Well, I'm glad at least the father is here. Can we begin?"

Helen's small and fragile new family gathers around the baptismal font. She looks up at the suffering Christ hanging over the altar. *I suppose it can be worse* is all that comes to her mind.

Danny rocks on his feet as if he were back on the trawler in rough seas. He's trying to figure out how he got so drunk so quick. It wasn't part of the plan for the day. But it wasn't an accident either. He looks at the priest, blathering away in a foreign tongue. hat the hell is he saying?

Then he looks down at the twin boys, Jack and Bobby. Who the hell are they? He had avoided thinking about them until they showed up one day. Born right in the bed where he sleeps. *The devil and his twin right in my fucking bed—where I sleep.* The whole time Helen was pregnant, he treated her pregnancy like an illness. His thoughts were about the future in America, not the nightmare of the past. And that future didn't include these two. Now the reality hits him like a prize fighter's punch to the gut. Helen holds Bobby while Margie hangs on to Jack. Danny keeps his hands in his pockets. He won't have any part of touching them. It's been that way from the beginning.

Helen stares at Danny, shutting out the ceremony taking place around her. She's never seen him so drunk. Sure, she watched him have a few pints at a dance, and they'd drunk a half bottle of whiskey that day, but he never staggered or slurred his words. This is a different person next to her. It's in his eyes. A distant, soulless look. But fuck him, she thinks. It happened to me. These are the shite cards we were dealt. Is this the man who is going to act like a husband and father, or is he just another self-pitying drunk penniless poet?

Sitting in the pew a few rows back is the daughter of one of Margie's friends, Mary, cheerful-looking lass with a little girl in hand. She recognizes the look on Danny, staggering on his feet, fists clenched, scowl on his face. If he's anything like her own husband, he'll be on his bike at the first opportunity. Poor girl, Mary thinks. I wish I could help her, but I don't think she's the type for my kind of work. Father Xavier certainly wouldn't approve. But a girl has to eat.

Danny looks over at Helen. The invisible angel on his shoulder leads his mind back to when he first met her. She had deep blue eyes, and her smile could melt his heart. On the dance floor, the touch of her hand brought him to his knees. She listened to his poetry. Good or bad, she would listen patiently. She let his verse caress her body, hold her hands, make her legs vibrate, fill her with desire. He loved that. She owned more than his heart. Helen held his soul in the palm of her hand.

Then he looks down at the twin devils, and his dream turns to a nightmare, the mortal embodiment of that day on the pond. Two new souls are put on this earth to remind Danny how impotent he is. Every day they walk, they will remind him how incapable he is to control his life, never mind protect those he loves. Worse, they ask the ugly question that haunts him the most. Somewhere between hero and coward is a victim. Was the horrible truth, that, if possible, Danny would have run? Was he a coward in the guise of a victim? Did the soldiers save him from showing his true self? Which way would he have gone? Hard questions to ask. Worse to answer. He never had the chance to find out what he was made of.

"Abrenuntias, Satan?" Father Xavier's voice drifts into focus.

Danny's head snaps to attention at the name of Satan. Let's blame him and those bastards and the fucking king. Is he at the root of this?

The priest waits for a response but only gets a blank look from Margie. Like a ventriloquist, he responds himself. "Abrenuntio."

Danny's eyes widen as he watches the priest anoint the infants. He can splash them in all the holy water he wants, but it won't wash away the sin, the stain of their conception. *Why do I have to pay for the sins of the dead? Why does Helen have to bear their curse?* Now thiss strange priest allows them to be a part of the holy church. *Satan's own, walking the aisles of God's holy church with impunity. Blasphemy.* Danny's mind spins out of control.

"Ego te baptizo in nomine Patris, et Filii, et Spiritus Sancti." Father Xavier sniffs back a fount of nasal drip and chokes out, "I baptize thee in the name the Father and of the Son and of the Holy

Ghost."

Unseen on Danny's shoulder sits the devil, pushing him along rage's sharpened edge. Images of that dog-faced sergeant and that other English son of a bitch flash through his mind. He can still hear Helen screaming. The invisible demon comes close to Danny's ear, like a mosquito ready to steal some blood. *What are you going to do about it? Where is the justice in all this? Why do you have to pay? You didn't kill anyone. Now you're a ghost in a strange land. For what? Two little English bastards?*

Danny's pulse quickens. Beads of sweat start to rain down from his temples. He looks the twins over. The little bastards have brown eyes. There is nothing like him in them. How can he ever live through the charade that pride forced on him?

You're not lashed now. The devil whispers in Danny's ear. *Nothing is holding you back.* Danny looks up at the crucified Christ hanging above the altar.

"Agh, you got off easy." Danny says to the carved wooden figure, perhaps a bit too loud. Father Xavier gives him a look. *Christ never experienced the humiliation of watching your best love ...* he can't even think the word without starting to cry. He'd trade places on the cross rather than endure all that's happened since then. Now Satan's own are members of the family and the Church.

No llonger able to hold back his emotions, Danny lashes out. "Nobody's holding me now!"

Danny's foot flies against the baptism font. Aunt Margie goes down in a heap, dropping Jack. Helen spins around like a ballet dancer, clutching Bobby, and avoids the font. The good reverend lands on his bottom in shock. Danny's foot begins to throb in pain. The marble baptismal font hits the marble floor and shatters to rubble.

The scene is witnessed and tried on the spot by the neighborhood hens.

I said they are trouble Never seen such a spectacle Imagine living with such an animal In the church In front of the priest.

I SAID NO TALKING.

"What in god's name came into you, man." Father Xavier throws Danny's helping hands off and rights himself. "God may forgive you, but I want you to pay for the font and never come back into my church." The priest regains his dignity.

"Now get out of my sight, the lot of you." Father Xavier looks over a family with more problems than he can ever hope to mend. Give the Presbyterians a try, he wants to say, but manages to hold his tongue.

In the back of the nave, the two men from the Cats' Eye Pub move through the shadows past the Stations of the Cross, casting judgment of their own. They know enough and have seen enough of Danny. He's not cut out for any further use to their friends in the old country.

"Put him on the list down at the loading docks. That's all he's good for."

Standing over the marble shattered baptism font, alone, is Danny. Worse is yet to come.

"I think I'm going to be sick."

10: February, 1918: Baltimore

Helen walks along snowy Lexington Street, investigating all the shops. There's a china shop with a beautiful window display. She sees dinnerware and crystal spread out on a table as if guests are expected. The setting takes her back to her childhood home, a pleasant cottage with a thatched roof and a pretty garden. Mother set a lovely table. Her father made a fair living caring for the horses on the Harriss estate. As the only child, she suffered little want. She played with the boys the clandestine field games like hurling and Gaelic football. Her spirit ran free and easy.

In the shop some elegant silverware is for sale, very ornate, very classy looking. Eating holiday meals with it would be wonderful. But right now a few tin spoons will have to do. Besides, her hands are full.

She comes to another beautiful shop. It's filled with colorful clothing. Bright blues, pinks, yellows, and reds that show no wartime apology. Perhaps the brightness is also a way of saying Fuck off to the Spanish Flu she keeps hearing about. Fur collars and hems on coats seem in fashion. They look warm. Dresses that sparkle like stars demand a night out dancing. All the clothing is lovely. Helen looks at her worn-out clothes. They're what she wore when she came here from Ireland. Whatever color her clothes may have had, the salt air from the Atlantic Ocean stole. Her outer layers have a stained salt look and feel stiff no matter how much they're washed. Her feet are frozen. Her shoes are scuffed and leak water. The heels are worn down. The laces are thin as spiderwebs, barely keeping them on her feet.

To Helen, the real color is out here, walking on the streets. This is nothing like her tiny village in Donegal. Even Belfast is a place where everyone looks like her cousin, including the Protestants. Here in her new home, in a new country, in a new big city, she feels alone. Other than Danny and a few relatives, she is an island unto herself and her responsibilities.

This is Lexington Street in Baltimore. Another port town like Belfast, except a bit more colorful. The Great War never visited here. She hears that the Spanish Flu was cruel to Baltimore but that the plague is going away. The roads are newly paved, the markets have fresh food. On the streets walk all manner of humans she never set eyes on in Donegal, why, there are Africans and Chinese on the same road. In the market on Lexington Street,

German, Italian, Greek, Polish, Russian, Yiddish prattle on in a stream of gibberish. No Gaelic, it seems. The aromas of exotic foods merge, making her sneeze.

She rolls her way up Lexington St. to the Mayfair Theatre. The marquee advertises the latest movie, "Broken Blossoms," starring Lillian Gish. She would love to go in and spend the afternoon in another world. One that's dark and safe, with a big velvet seat to fall into. She needs only a good piano player to transport her to another reality. The world on the big screen is filled with heroes defeating villains, good over evil, an ordered universe that never fails.

The poster of Lillian Gish looks at Helen, daring comparison. Helen thinks they have the same round face and smoldering eyes, but their hair is different. Helen strokes her long dark hair over her shoulder. She winds it around in her hand, trying to match the movie star's curls.

"Broken Blossoms" promises a story of platonic and unrequited love. Of oppression from the authority figure, a drunken father; a futile attempt by a near-hero to save the damsel. A Chinese Buddhist. She would love to go in and stay for the show, but she has other priorities.

Back in the old country, Helen was a prize student. There was talk of her going to Trinity if she could get the right recommendations and some help with expenses. At worst, she thought, she'd work in a shop. Danny would work at the newspaper, and they'd live happily ever after. Then there is Danny. She hopes she still loves him. The past few years have not been kind to the newlyweds. His dreams change like the weather. But here they are now, in Somewhere, USA. Anywhere but home.

On the corner near the trolley stop is Gottfried Fine Millinery. The latest styles are on display. She ventures in. One hat particularly attracts Helen. It's hunter green, shaped like a triangle, swept back to a point on top. There's a white plume on the side and a black veil that hangs down to cover the face. Helen can't stop herself from trying it on. She looks like an Alpine huntress. When the veil falls over her face, Helen feels safe as in the confines of a confessional. Peering out from the veil to the mirror, she sees a mysterious and glamorous reflection, and she likes it. Looking around to make sure nobody is looking, Helen poses in front of the mirror like a movie star on a poster. She stares into the mirror, imagining a close-up. Her face is pleasant enough. High cheekbones sprinkled with light freckles keep the flame of girlhood alive. Helen practices making big doe eyes for the camera. It's in her eyes that her adult anxiety hides.

"Miss, may I help you?" An officious clerk, a middle-aged towering wraith of a woman, approaches Helen, looking down her nose at her.

"Oh no, ma'am. I was just admiring the hat." Helen places the hat back on the shelf. Suddenly she realizes how foreign she sounds.

The wraith walks around Helen, taking in a good look.

"That ring, on your hand. It's exquisite."

"I beg your pardon. My husband gave it to me for our wedding." Helen glares at the woman. "It's from Harrods—that's in London. Have you heard of it?"

"Yes, of course. It just looks like something—let's say, out of your reach. It must have taken his last penny. I'm sure he's very much in love. Now, unless you intend to make a purchase, I'm going to have to ask you to leave." The clerk stands with one shoulder forward as if she is ready to parry. She does not trust foreigners.

"How much is the hat?" Helen extends her hand so her beautiful ring can be seen in the best light.

"Come now. Let's not embarrass each other." The clerk points down at Helen's feet with a sneer. "And please take those with you."

"It's a—them, not a—those." Helen knows what the woman is talking about. "Ma'am."

"Nevertheless. Please see yourself out. I have customers to attend." The clerk turns around with military precision and greets her clients. "Ah, welcome, ladies. So good to see you."

Helen glares at the clerk. She raises her arm with a mock pistol in her hand and takes aim at the back of the clerk's head. With one eye closed, she takes careful aim. "Bang."

Helen laughs. It's always a matter of opportunity, so she waits. The veins in her head pulsate. The clerk is busy kowtowing to the women from uptown, fat prattling old women in well-tailored clothes. Helen can hear them chatting about the tribulations of the wealthy class: the demanding poor, unreliable help, and taxes. While the sales banshee has her back turned, Helen strikes. She tosses the hat into the bag at her feet, scoops everything up, and pushes out the door.

Her heart pounds as if it could break a rib, but she feels so good. Almost like when she… *Do not finish that thought,* she says to herself.

Once safely down the street, Helen slows down. She's been pushing a wicker pram with precious cargo through mud and snow and is exhausted. She can hear music playing from a shop door, above the din of the city crowd. Moving toward the music, she thinks of a church. At home she went to mass devoutly on Sundays, not to mention daily Mass in school. The last time she was in a church was a debacle. The hymn-like music leads her to Sweggler and Son Bible and Religious Emporium.

The shop window displays bibles, crucifixes, paintings of Jesus in different sizes and scenes. But for Helen the biggest attraction is the Help Wanted sign.

Helen pushes her pram through the door. It's a small shop, narrow and long. The walls are lined with gold-painted Christian art and jewelry. It seems Jesus has eyes everywhere, watching, from the paintings to cheap ceramic statues in his likeness.

"May I help you, young lady?" The man isn't just rotund; he is a planet unto himself. He has fat cheeks and jowls that change shape when he smiles. His head is balding and reeks of the pomade holding the last defiant hair in place. He's built like Humpty Dumpty: a plaid suit, little arms, undersized legs, the whole body wrapped with a belt around the middle.

"I heard the music, then saw the sign. I thought maybe it's a—sign—from above." Helen attempts a smile while pointing toward heaven. "So to speak. The Help Wanted sign."

Helen indicates the sign. She tries to take a step back from the counter, but the girth of the man forces her against the shelves.

"Pardon me. It's a small shop. Let me call Sister. I need her say before I hire anyone. Oh, Sister!" The fat man turns to Helen, sweat pouring off his brow. He wipes himself down with a huge well-used handkerchief. "She's not really my sister. We are married. Husband and wife. But we are Brother and Sister in the Fellowship of the Suffering Jesus."

As fat as Brother is, Sister is thin. She barely casts a shadow, yet her voice has a piercing staccato quality that assaults the ears.

"What do you want?"

"I came to inquire about the position."

"Dear God. Where is that accent from?" The woman holds her ears as if in pain.

"I'm from Ireland, the West, Donegal. A small little place." Helen attempts to be charming. After all, isn't that what the Irish are known for?

"Enough. You're making my ears hurt. I don't need to know any more. You're a papist, aren't you?" Sister accuses. "Popery. Catholic. Well?"

Helen can only nod, confused by the questions. She thought she was in a country this sort of thing was left behind.

"Bad enough she's a papist, she's Irish. They carry pestilence. They brought the Flu. They're filthy, look at her."

Helen looks herself over. She may not be a boardwalk beauty contestant, but she is well groomed. Her hair is combed, face washed, clothes mended—what else does Sister want?

"Now, Sister. She seems to be a sweet young lady." Brother strokes Helen's cheek like a parent. "Let me show her around. If she is strong enough to handle the top shelf merchandise without falling, I say we give her a chance."

"No. I can smell the sick on her." Sister sniffs around, clenching her nose. "It's coming from this contraption."

Sister puts her nose to the pram. "What's in here that can smell so vile?"

Helen rolls her eyes. She's been out for a long time and needs to take care of some business. She pushes the rude woman out of the way. There is a blanket covering the wicker pram. Helen pulls it down.

"This is Bobby, and this is Jack," Helen reveals her twin boys, barely a year old. One of them has shit escaping the diaper and out his pants.

"Oh, the smell. See. They live in their own filth. Irish Catholics breed like rabbits. They are ill-tempered, uneducated, unskilled, untrustworthy. She is probably a Communist or worse, a Democrat. They are a drain on society. They need to be rounded up and shipped back to where they came from. Or Canada. I'd rather hire a Negro. At least they don't talk as much as the Irish."

"Thank you, Ma'am, your kindness is like listening to Jesus himself." Helen glares at the woman. She pulls the cross out from inside her shirt.

"I don't mean to be rude. It's just that our customers are God-fearing Christians who don't abide by the corrupt Pope and are aware that foreigners carry disease." This is as close to an apology as Sister can muster.

"Sister. I hate to interrupt. Let's see if she still wants the job after seeing the rest of the shop."

Like a steamship in a tight harbor, Brother turns around the counter and into the narrow hallway.

"Follow me, Miss. Sister, please be kind enough to watch God's little creatures for a moment." Brother waddles through the passage and stops at the storeroom entrance.

"This way, please." Brother smiles and points the way with his tiny arm.

Helen moves cautiously. She looks Sister over, hoping the woman won't harm her kids. The narrow hall is dimly lit, only stray daylight showing the way. The walls are lined with overstocked shelves. From the dust, Helen thinks sales are less than brisk.

"This is the storeroom. See how you do on the step stool." Brother is all smiles. He has the demeanor of a church choirmaster.

Helen looks into the room, more of a closet. Floor to ceiling, it's packed with books, art, jewelry—all with the suffering Jesus them

"Go ahead, step up and see what you can reach." Brother follows Helen in.

She turns around and sees Brother blocking the doorway. Helen imagines how Jesus felt when they rolled the boulder in front of the tomb. Turning back to the step stool, she hikes her skirt up enough not to trip and climbs to the top. Brother leans his face in towards Helen's bottom. He takes a deep breath, inhaling like a sommelier examining a bottle of wine. Helen looks down and sees him, eyes shut, nose inches from her.

"Excuse me, sir." Helen climbs down. "What are you doing?"

"I'm inhaling your purity." Brother answers. "I can tell how pure a soul is by its genital scent. It is not a science as much as a gift. To work here, I will have to know the purity of your soul."

"Will you take my word for it if I tell you?"

"It's just that after childbirth, well, you know. It's such a violation of the flesh. But I guess the flesh is violated to get with child in the first place. Of course, Sister would never allow such a violation. Is the child of lust or love? I must find out for myself," Brother continues, seeming with all sincerity. "Now if I can take a deep breath of your womanhood, I would much be obliged."

Brother doesn't wait for Helen's answer and begins to lift her skirt. His hands ride up Helen's thighs. A swift kick to Brother in the balls is her first thought. That slows any man down. But, with the girth of him, she can't see them. Helen makes a fist as hard as a hammer.

Outside the storeroom, Sister glares at Jack and Bobby. No longer asleep, the boys want to get out of the pram. They're squirming around covered in shit. Sister finds a fireplace poker and uses it like a lion tamer, prodding the boys back into the pram.

There is a sudden smash and what feels like an earthquake. Brother crashes backward out of the storeroom. Helen stands over him like a trophy hunter.

"Tell me what a lady wants to hear," Helen demands from Brother.

"Get off me, I'm going to throw up." Brother groans and curls into a fetal position.

"Call yourself a Christian. A trip to the confessional wouldn't hurt." Helen crosses over the floundering hulk and takes command of her pram.

Before she walks out the door, she takes the stolen hat from her bag and places it snugly on her head. She pulls the veil across her face and takes one last contemptuous look at Sister and her vomiting Brother.

Back out on the street, Helen finds comfort in the crowd. She starts her trip home. The boys need a bath, and their clothes should be burned. A few blocks down Lexington Street to Howard Street, they pass Hutzler's window displays. Helen slows and looks at the children's clothing. There is a small seaside scene. A pier, with a painted beach and sky, sets the stage for two mannequins in little sailor suits. Helen looks at her boys in their ill-fitting, dirty gowns that make them look like little girls. She fantasizes her boys sailing a dinghy on a pristine pond, commanders of their own destiny. The boys can have their own adventures and make their dear mother proud. Helen closes her eyes and dreams of her little men, her little navy floating onto the pond that day. Their guns blazing, they chase the Brits away, saving the day for Mommy and Daddy.

The cries of dirty, hungry boys snap Helen back to the present. It's a long walk, but they do it in record time.

"I didn't hear you. Where have you been?" Danny comes to the door, unshaven, pants open and falling down. "I was just sleeping."

"Just sleeping it off, more like it." Helen leaves the pram outside the apartment. She unloads the boys, who duckwalk their way inside with their loaded nappies.

"What did you do today?" Danny asks.

"Nothing much. I did get a lovely new hat." Helen shows off her trophy.

"What? Ahh. Nothing for us to drink or eat?"

"No."

"Shite."

11: November, 1918: Aunt Margie's apartment, Baltimore

Helen sips from a cup of tea. She stares, expressionless, at the little twins, rolling around on the floor. They're good now, but soon their bellies will be empty, and the crying and the fidgeting will begin. Helen goes into the kitchen and stares at the cupboard, hoping for a miracle to appear. Even the mice seem to have left in despair.

She looks over at Danny. He's in his usual state: an inarticulate stupor, next to a blank page and a bottle of whiskey. He's been like this since the twins were born. All his ambitions and dreams find their way down his throat. He barely talks to anyone. When he does, she wishes he'd shut up. Forget the kids—he can't look at them.

Helen is beyond crying. This is her life. Christ, that smell is in the air. A nappy needs changing. She moves without emotion. The day of picking the children up with gentleness and affection are over. She tosses the offending child on the table like a sack of potatoes.

"I know it's hard." Aunt Margie puts her hand on Helen's shoulder. "But this can't go on much longer."

Helen nods in agreement. She and her boys have been staying too long with her aunt in America, in Baltimore. If she didn't have a price on her head, she would rather be poor in Belfast than in this wretched city plagued with poverty and sickness.

"Look, I know you had to get married in a rush." Aunt Margie wrings her hands. "I'm not stupid, I don't know what you did besides getting knocked up, but I know you had trouble with the Crown. You know what they did to your father?" Helen knows exactly what happened. The soldiers came looking for her and Danny. "They beat the old man almost to death. In front of your mother, no less.

"How could you get in a fix like that? At your age? Dear God, you're hardly twenty. It usually takes a long time to get in this much trouble. But we're family, and this is what families do for each other." Helen's aunt holds up her finger to make a dramatic point. "But—I'm an aunt two or three times removed, and this is America. What happens in Ireland, well, nobody really gives a shit."

Helen says nothing. Her eyes swing between the young boys and her husband.

"I like Danny well enough, but he can't keep drinking your uncle's booze. Besides, you haven't paid any rent, and the boys are getting bigger and your…" Aunt Margie tries to explain, but Helen cuts her off.

"I know we need to make it on our own." Helen turns her back on her aunt. There's a thud from the other room. She looks over with casual interest. Danny has fallen off his chair and lies passed out on the floor next to the boys. "I don't know what to do."

"You poor thing. I have a friend. You're not going to like what I'm suggesting, but when times are bad and with that accent of yours, and the city still afraid of foreigners, I don't know what other options you have." Her aunt can't look her in the eye.

12: November, 1918: Helen's career opportunities

The next night, Aunt Margie's friend arrives with information and an invitation to the free enterprise system in America.

"Hello, dearie. So you'd like to join me in the trade." She's a stout young woman whose makeup looks as if it had been applied at a carnival.

"You must be Mary? You were at the baptism." Helen's aunt has second thoughts about what she is asking her of Helen. "You are looking for Helen, my niece."

Helen is half hiding behind the kitchen door, hoping not to be seen.

"Aye, I am. But they call me Fast Mary. I get the job done in a hurry, if you know what I mean." Fast Mary gives Helen a wink that shoots by her, meaningless. "In, out. Next. That's what I say. This ain't the barber's."

Aunt Margie laughs out of embarrassment.

"So let's get a look at you." Fast Mary gives Helen a head-to-toe assessment and shakes her head. "You're going to wear something else. Right. Think of it as work clhes."

Fast Mary takes charge like a battle-tested veteran. She finds a flimsy nightgown among Helen's pathetic trousseau. Fast Mary digs into her work bag, stuffed with cleanup rags, a bottle of gin, a knife, and makeup. Using the bold strokes of a billboard painter, Fast Mary transforms Helen.

"Have you thought about cutting your hair in a bob? I think you'd look adorable." Fast Mary lifts Helen's long hair, trying to imagine it short.

"Right. Let's get on with it." Fast Mary takes Helen by the hand. Helen plants her feet.

"I understand the first time is tough. But it's not like you've never done it before. You're just doing it to someone you don't know."

Helen looks over at her babies, sitting with Aunt Margie. Except for that … She can't finish the thought. She's never. Even with Danny. They were very young and just started courting when everything happened. She was a good girl, and Danny was a good lad. He even asked her Da for permission to take her on that picnic. The idea of strangers having their way like the … only for money … is beyond Helen's imagination.

Fast Mary leads—drags—Helen to the park. It's a small green space shaped like a triangle, separating Pigtown and the Otterbein from the swells of Bolton Hill. Gaslights never made it here. So much the better for carnal arts best practiced in the dark. The shadows grant a certain equality to the women who work the park.

"Who's he?" Helen points to a flamboyant bronze soldier on horseback.

"That's General Robert E. Lee," Fast Mary answers. "He led the Rebel Army during the War between the States."

"Did he win?" Helen wonders.

"No."

"Why the statue then?"

Fast Mary shrugs.

As they walk past the statue, a different world reveals itself. Helen looks up at General Lee and sees him as the sentry to vice and debauchery. In each shadow, each corner, each opening in the hedges, waits a woman for sale. The sun has closed up shop and the moon is in charge. Temptation's market is open. The women come out onto the cobblestone and show off their wares. Helen is amazed how little is needed to seduce men. Breasts, backsides, legs—everything is advertised. She fidgets with her clothes, trying to copy what she sees. Shyly, she lets her shawl fall off her shoulder, revealing her young neck.

Like sheep walking through a convention of wolves, Helen and Fast Mary pass through the park. Helen can feel predators' eyes violating her. Barks and whistles assault her, along with requests for acts a nice Catholic girl from western Ireland never heard of.

"Don't worry about the fancy-name things. Stick to two things, fucking and sucking. Keep it to one at a time. You'll be fine." Fast Mary senses Helen getting overwhelmed. "Oh, and carry some protection. Like a knife or a gun or something."

"Is this what you're going to do?" Helen feels as if she is outside her body.

"You get used to it." A flask of gin appears from Fast Mary's purse. She downs a swig. She offers the flask to Helen.

"No thanks." Helen declines but understands.

"A spot of this helps. But a girl has to do what a girl has to do. My kid's father disappeared years ago. At least yours is still around. You have hope." Fast Mary gives Helen a pat on the back. "Here's a spot. Just watch me."

Helen falls into the shadows to watch Fast Mary ply her trade. It's not long before a man walks up to her. Fast Mary brings a swagger up to the gentleman. Hands on hips, she bends over to best display her bosom. The gentleman gives them a squeeze like a fruit inspector. Fast Mary leads him by the hand into the dark. He leans against a tree trunk and lets Fast Mary do all the work. She runs her hands down his nice suit coat and unbuckles his pants. Dropping to her knees, Fast Mary earns her street name.

Helen's eyes are as wide as a cat's. Her teacher gives a knowing glance from her knees. Two shakes of a lamb's tail, a gentleman's groan, and it's over. Fast Mary coughs and spits. The gentleman gives her some coins and disappears into the night without a word.

"Cold fucking night in hell. I can't do that," Helen says in a panic.

"Relax, hon. It's not that tough." Fast Mary can't remember her first time. It seems like a century ago. She opens her hand and shows Helen how much money she made in only a few minutes. "Just open wide, close your eyes, and count coins."

"Oh, Jesus." Helen shakes her head. This is far beyond Father Octopus groping schoolgirls in the rectory at St. Brendan's.

"We'll talk later. Here comes a regular." Fast Mary fixes her hair. Wipes her mouth and refreshes with another swig of gin.

"Hey, baby. Where have you been? I've been so lonely." The regular seems happy to see her. "Mary, Mary, I've so much to tell you. Take me somewhere wonderful. I'll tell you all about ….." He is an older fellow, a few sheets to the wind, wearing a raincoat on a clear night.

Fast Mary looks at Helen and rolls her eyes.

"You may want to go get a cup of coffee. This is going to take a while," Fast Mary whispers.

"Let's go, lover." Fast Mary leads her regular into the dark and finds a tree to brace against.

Helen tours the park on her own. Like moths to a gaslight, men start approaching her. Whistles, barks, kissing sounds as well as straightforward propositions come her way. She realizes getting attention isn't hard. The sea of loneliness is well-stocked. She has only to cast her net. A cupboard full of fresh food, new clothes, maybe some toys for the babies, all exist in her imagination waiting to become a reality. All she has to do is close her eyes, open wide, and count coins.

The statue of the rebel leader, with his righteous raised sword, acts as a beacon for those with unmet desires. It's nicely secluded by shrubs and has benches providing comfort for whatever is required. Helen watches a nameless, faceless couple engage in loveless sex. She inches closer to hear small parcels of conversation. The woman runs together a string of cliches and what sound like orders. She praises the Lord and admires the man's physical size and girth. Meanwhile the man needs to know how much she desires it and how much it pleases her. Helen thinks it sounds like a lack of confidence on his part. What surprises Helen most is that the woman can perform, orate, and still manage a cigarette. She must be a skilled professional.

Helen watches them grind against each other in an inelegant ballet. What compels two strangers to behave so? To be so intimate and still so far apart. It's nothing like love. What drives men to seek such carnal release without love, without a poet's passion, without emotion? Is there such emptiness in them that they live for that brief moment of exhilaration? That one split second when their existence is announced to an uncaring universe when they scream—I came—*I am*. He doesn't want her love. Helen senses that he feeds the void in his soul with the carnage of flesh. For the woman, Helen knows all too well, rape or purchase are the same. Only one is profitable.

Her chances of romantic love with Danny died that day in Ireland. She needs to move on and feed her children. If this is the way, so be it.

"Hey sister, if you want to watch, go to the movie house." Helen blushes when she is found out.

"All right, you're done. Get off me." The pro slides the customer off her, hand out, palm up to Helen. "Who the fuck are you? I've never seen you here before. Hey not so fast, pay up, bucko."

"I—I—I…." Helen is lost for words.

"Didn't mean to ask such a hard question. How about this? Is the fucking circus in town? What are you dressed up as?" The whore moves around Helen, taking her for what she is. A little girl in drab clothes, trying to act the part of a woman selling sex. "This is my part of the park. Nobody comes here but me and my johns. Little sister, you best go back to that convent you came from. You're not cut out for this."

Helen decides the woman under the statue is right and runs off in the dark searching for Fast Mary.

13: Trip to the pawn shop

The sun's been up for a while. Helen hides under the blanket. Danny snores next to her and the twins fill in the small space between them. She doesn't want to move for fear of waking any of them up. Margie is clanging about. The boys will wake hungry and Danny will be holding his aching head barking at everyone.

Last night was awful. Helen tries to forget what she saw. How could she? She tries to imagine herself doing those things. Impossible. There must be another way. Staring at the ceiling, Helen hopes the chipped plaster will offer a plan. She spins her wedding band on her finger with nervous energy. Each spin seems to point in the direction of last chances.

"Margie, shhh. Don't wake them for as long as you can. I'll be back with something to eat." Helen sneaks out of bed and tiptoes across the apartment.

"Where are you going? Don't leave me with these three."

"Frank will help you when he gets up," Helen says.

"Ha. He would have to be here to help." The mention of Frank's name puts Margie in a worse mood.

Helen cringes, not ready to take on someone else's burden. She is too busy shouldering her own. She heads for the door and places her hat smartly on her head.

It's almost noon and Lexington Street is bustling. Near the market, people move shoulder to shoulder. The walking is easier a few blocks down where the retail and pawnshops beg attention. Helen takes her time passing the shop windows. Dreams on display. Some windows show Helen dreams she didn't know she had. Clothes, jewelry, shoes, makeup, riches the world keeps out of her reach. There are so many dreams to choose from. She's not a little girl anymore, with little-girl aspirations. She can't have all these dreams, but if she could have one, what would it be?

Helen stops in front of Hutzler's. This particular display has been there for a long time, but she loves it, that seaside setting with two little sailor boys fishing on a pier. This is the one, the dream she locks up in her heart. Her two little sailors, brave and clean. Articulate young men of great wit and intelligence. Helen spins her wedding band on her finger. She sees them on seas of imagination. Maybe they will return to be liberators of the old country. Maybe they are Americans and will be heroes in those games they play here. Down the street, the shops that barter in fantasies are open for business. The profit margin lies in shards of broken dreams. Helen spins her wedding band until her finger is red as raw meat.

Pawnshop displays are simple. Merchandise sits in the window: you want it or not? No enticements, no offer of great value, no guarantee of happiness. Yes or no. Now, if you have a dream to sell, come in, someone will be right over to help you. The man behind the counter is either an angel or the Devil himself; that identity is in the eye of the customer. Helen spins her wedding band.

"Yup," he says without looking up.

Helen walks into the pawnshop feeling like a cat lost in a dog pound. The shop has an inventory of anything that can be picked up and carried in, from grandfather clocks to pocket watches, embroidered sofas to wooden folding chairs to tiny embroidered footstools. Handwritten tags show their value.

"I have something to sell." Helen's voice is barely above a whisper.

"Huh?"

"To sell. I have something to sell." Helen manages a little more conviction. Her finger starts to hurt but she can't stop spinning the damn ring.

"What?" The counterman is annoyed. He drops the racing forms he was reading. There is more on a horse in the seventh than this ring is worth. He would rather do anything other than give this little foreigner the time of day. "Let's see it."

Helen takes the band off her finger. She doesn't know what Danny did to get it. She can't imagine what the IRB had him do. Whatever it was, there was a high price paid. She gives it a final look and gives it a kiss.

Without looking at the counterman, she hands over her wedding band for his judgment. He takes out a jeweler's glass and looks over the ring. There is an inscription inside the band.

There is but one love.

Out of her pocket she pulls a simple strand of twine, limp and worn. Helen wraps the twine around her finger. She lets the frayed edges cut into her flesh. The counterman pays her no attention, only holding the ring up to better light, then scratching his chin. There are some papers on the counter with gold and silver prices. She leaves him to his calculations.

Helen wanders the shop. So many guitars, banjos, violins—an orchestra could be outfitted here. Something shiny catches her eye. Helen goes to see it up close and it strikes her as strange to see in a pawnshop. It has to be stolen. Do churches go out of business? Maybe there is a market for religion on the cheap. It's a communion chalice, sitting on a shelf with nothing around it to indicate its sanctity.

The last time Helen saw a communion chalice, or saw the inside of a church, was when the boys were baptized. That was the first time she saw Danny drunk. She was never sure what put Danny over the edge.

Helen remembers they were there—Danny, herself, and Margie at St. Mary's. The boys in little baptism gowns, looking as innocent as newborns can be. Helen never understood how the church can talk of original sin and the innocence of babies in one breath. Bobby and Jack were as innocent as any two creatures. They didn't ask to be created. They didn't beg the universe for breath. Yet here they are. Now what happens? Will destiny be as cruel to them? Helen makes the twine tighter on her finger. When the holy water was splashed on their heads, they did not burst into flames as the Devil was expelled. When the cross was rubbed onto their foreheads, they did not scream in pain. Was this because of a dismissive, uncaring God? Or maybe there's no Devil to deny? Once sanctified by baptismal water, they were made "real." Part of the tribe. The Devil was invited into the house. Someone had to go, so Danny left with a bottle under his arm.

What did make them cry were empty tummies and nasty nappies. The only thing that will end those is cash. All the Hail Marys and Our Fathers combined won't put cash in her pocket or food on the table.

"So how much?"

14: Helen goes to the park

"It's not that hard." Fast Mary is getting frustrated with Helen. "Just one foot out front, bend your hip. Shit, just relax."

Helen tries a variety of poses to entice men. So far she has only discovered self-torturing bends and stretches. She sees herself as a yogi from a Kipling story.

"You'll figure it out. It's not like sharks are picky eaters." Fast Mary shakes her head. "I'll send some over to you. Just don't take my regulars. It took a long time to break them in."

Helen nods. She feels like a human sacrifice being led to a fiery pyre.

"I'm not ready. Let me walk around." Helen throws her hands up. She's going to need a running start to make the leap.

Walking around isn't helping. Her eyes are used to the dark. She can see through the shadows. It was better when it was just darkness. So much for the mystery of the erotic arts. Her stroll through the park is an education. She takes her forefinger and puts it in her mouth. Back and forth in tentative mimicry. Then she tries her thumb. A simple childhood pleasure now tarnished.

"You." A man's voice calls from the dark.

Helen points to herself and looks around to see if there is another saleswoman on the floor.

"Yeah. You." He steps into the light. Helen liked him better in the shadow.

"Oh. Um. You see. I …" So small talk isn't her forte.

"You know what I want?" He takes another step closer.

Not a wild guess.

"You know, I think you're looking for someone else. If I may direct you that way. Ask for Mary."

"Sure, if that's the game. Thanks, sister."

Dear God, that was close. Helen feels as if she survived a train crash.

The statue of General Lee catches Helen's attention. The oversized figure of man and horse are truly inspired by male preoccupations. The size of the horse's cock is either an artistic boast or wishful thinking.

Under the statue is the park's best teacher or businesswoman. She must be. This is the best spot in the park. It has its own enclosure of hedges. Stone benches, if not comfortable, are handy. The woman who works this spot must have done something right. Helen decides to study at the foot of the master.

Helen takes a seat on one of the benches. She's quiet, as if she's in church. In front of her is performed an act she's seen done everywhere in the park. So far nothing special. There is a common rhythmic pattern. It seems pretty simple. One, two, one, two. Legs in the air, or feet on the ground—hardly a dance.

"Are you back?" The whore sees Helen sitting politely on the bench. "Didn't I chase you off?"

The whore lights up a smoke. The match light reveals a woman past her prime. Makeup doesn't fill the tracks time carved into her face.

"Get the fuck out of here, little sister." The whore shoves Helen, two-handed. "You don't belong. Go back to that fucking place you came from, little sister."

The whore takes another step toward Helen.

"This is my spot. Fuck off." The whore launches a mighty ball of spit that splats on Helen's feet. "Now fuck off before you get hurt. Little sister."

"Little sister, eh?" Helen looks at her tattered shoes, stained black and yellow with this vile woman's spit. A spark set is to a fuse; Helen is ready to fight. The spark runs straight past her brain and to the primal animal that lives within her. "You think you own this corner of the park?"

Helen shows no fear, but inside, her heart pounds. She holds her ground. Whether it's destiny or free choice, it's right here, right now, that Helen's future is being written. The option to walk away eludes her.

"I do." The statue whore moves toward Helen with the intent to intimidate the newcomer.

Helen looks the woman over, nothing special in size or beauty. Her Dutch Boy haircut gives her a stern look. Bags under the eyes and lines around the mouth expose her time on the street. She wears a faded floozy costume that drapes loosely over her body. The whore's tits sag. Helen holds her own tits, still high with youth.

Without a King's regiment behind her, the whore is powerless. The woman doesn't know what this little sister is capable of. She doesn't know she is talking to a hero in the eyes of the Irish Republican fucking Brotherhood. Does this woman think she's going to frighten off someone who had been running from one safe house to another, death a step behind clad in royal red? She has another think coming.

The Celtic fire burns in Helen's heart. Challenge, ego, need, all reasons for Helen to take on this woman of the dark. What Helen doesn't take into account is who she's dealing with. A hardened street hooker forged in street violence.

A flash of light, then the pointed edge of a stiletto knife presses against Helen's windpipe.

"I don't think you'll be working around here, or anywhere else." The statue whore wields the knife like a butcher at the meat counter. She runs its blade down from Helen's ear to her jaw, just as if she were a butcher slicing beef. Helen doesn't realize what just happened until she sees blood dripping down to her shawl. The blade is surgical-sharp. It takes a moment for the pain to catch up to the wound.

"Jesus Christ." Helen holds her face, trying to stop the bleeding. Rage inside her roars like a furnace.

"Now get the fuck out of here. It seems I've got to teach a new girl every once in a while. This is my corner." The statue whore is proud of her victory. Her turf is safe, and there is one less net out fishing.

Helen's mind works through the pain. The best IRB commanders taught her a few lessons. Don't fight in a rage without a plan and don't fight without an advantage. Right now Helen has neither.

"That's it, go back to that hill in West Virginny or wherever you come from." Satisfied with her victory, the harlot walks over to the base of the statue. She rings a dinner bell, announcing she's open for business. Slowly the denizens of the night slither out to purchase her charms.

Helen walks in a storm to meet Fast Mary. Her heart races, her brain spins like a record on a Victrola.

"Where have you been? I don't mind fucking them, but holy shit if I had one rule it would be no talking. That asshole never stopped beating his gums. It takes twice as long with all that gibberish. I mean time is money, right?" Fast Mary stops Helen by the arm. "Sweet Jesus, what happened to you? First night out. Which one of these monsters did this?"

"Let me have a swig of that." Helen points to the flask of gin. Fast Mary quickly offers it up. "It wasn't a man."

Helen points over to the statue of General Lee.

"Oh no. I should've told you not to go there. An evil witch works there." Fast Mary shakes her head.

"Not for long." Helen takes another swig of gin.

15: November, 1918: Helen becomes Queen

"Dear, please don't go out tonight. We'll figure something out. You are going to get killed, or worse." Aunt Margie begs Helen not to get ready for another night out with Fast Mary. "Have you looked in a mirror?"

"I'll be fine." Helen looks in the mirror over the wash basin. The wound is fresh and still bleeds when the scab pulls apart. She should get stitches, but that would cost money she doesn't have. Helen takes her prized hat out of the closet. It looks sharp with the feather. She puts the hat on and frames the veil over the slash. She heard enough loose talk on the trawler to know little stops a man with a hard-on. The men don't even care if the women have all their limbs. All they care about is that sweet spot between their legs. A scar isn't stopping anyone. But it infuriates Helen. She doesn't want anyone to see her like this. And worse, it makes her special. Without a scar, she is another faceless streetwalker nobody will remember. With a scar, she becomes a story drunk men will tell for years. She doesn't want anyone remembering her this way.

Tonight she has a plan. It's simple, based on her hurling ability. Her uncle played. His old stick still stands in the closet. She holds the hurling stick, made of ash, its slender handle well-worn, perfected by years of competition. Its ladle-like head is perfect for smashing a skull, then scooping out the brains. Fast Mary shows up just as the sun disappears and the moon begins to rise. It looks like a clear, cool night. Perfect for Helen's plan.

"Are you all right, hon?" Mary comes into the bedroom uninvited. She goes straight to inspecting Helen's gash. "I hope this doesn't get infected. Put some petroleum jelly on it. At least it won't bleed so much."

Helen agrees and lets her new friend help.

"What's going on? Where you going?" Danny lumbers into the small bedroom. "Who the fuck are you?"

"Go sit down and watch the boys. Me and my friend are going to a temperance meeting." That should keep him wondering for a while.

"The who? Oh, right. The boys." Danny stumbles back into the sitting room. "What do I do with them?"

"Try feeding them, for God's sake. Change a diaper. Stop being so helpless. Margie, help him. We have to go." Helen shoos Mary, grabs the hurling axe, and slides it inside her shawl.

"What's that for? This isn't good. I think we should just stay away from there." Fast Mary doesn't share Helen's confident attitude.

Helen waves her hand for a swig of gin. Mary helps her out. The gin helps sort Helen's mind. She knows she's going to a winner-take-all fight. Looking around the room, she sees nothing but squalor, want, and need. There is nothing to lose. Dying tonight might be a blessing from God.

"Mary. Do you know what it feels like to kill someone?" Helen looks Mary in the eye but holds a smile. A mouthful of gin finds its way down her throat.

Mary wonders what happened to the shy immigrant girl from yesterday.

There are no words Helen can find to answer her own question. She holds her new friend by the shoulders. "Now let's go to work under our new spot."

Helen and Fast Mary make their way to the park. Helen walks in through the southern entrance to the General Lee terrace. Fast Mary stands behind her, uncertain what to do. The statue whore is engaged in trade, bent over the statue's base. She can't see who just entered her domain.

"I'll ring the bell when I'm ready. Wait your turn like everyone else. Tell them, big fella, I'm the best piece of ass in this shithole." She expects her rules to be respected.

The man grunts and pumps like a dog up on a bitch in heat.

"That's a nice piece of shagging you're doing. Good way to go out." Three weeks on a trawler gave Helen a salty vocabulary. She speaks loudly, hoping to be heard everywhere.

116

"Are you that stupid to come back?" The wicked whore spins, towing her john by the penis. She laughs at Helen's veil. "Ain't you pretty."

Helen speaks with authority. "I think it's time for this spot to be under new management. So why don't you pack up your gear and try Druid Hill or Patterson? From Mary, Helen has picked up a bit of knowledge about Baltimore neighborhoods open for business. "Starting tonight, this is mine."

"Do I have to cut you again?" The whore can't believe Helen is challenging her. It's magic time. A stiletto appears out of nowhere, while the john disappears. "This time I'm going to kill you."

A small audience builds at a distance. A few curious men gather, hoping for good entertainment. Dollars flash; let the wagering begin. Some of the working women expect to pick the loser's clothes. Fast Mary takes another gulp of gin and starts praying.

"You're not going to cut anyone again." Helen lets the hurley stick slide through her shawl and settle in her hand. "I grew up playing an old Irish game. It's called hurling. This stick is more natural in my hands than your father's limp little dick."

"Fuck you." The whore is still trying to figure out this insolent child.

"Now that this is my corner of the park and a small part of the bigger world, I have two rules. One, no talking, and two, I don't want to see you." Helen takes the hurling stick in two hands.

"You little bitch, coming here…" Before the whore can finish her thought, Helen launches the hurling stick into the whore's skull like a battle-axe. Spitting teeth, the statue whore falls. Helen stands over her enemy like the mighty Scáthach, Celtic warrior woman from Skye. There is no room for negotiations when both sides feel the righteous high ground.

"I said, no talking. Too many big words for you to understand." Helen uses the stick, poking to see if her enemy is still alive.

"Tell me what I want to hear." Helen steps out of her body and is watching a stranger take control. "Tell me what I fucking want to hear, and I won't beat you to death."

The whore is gathering her wits and searches for her knife. Helen sees the blade as well, flipping it on the stick's head and smacking it into the shrubs. Some of the working girls scramble for the weapon.

"I will toss your dead body in the gutter if you don't tell me what I want to hear." Helen is in full rage and has the advantage.

"What are you talking about?"

"Why is this so bloody hard to understand?" Helen gives her body over to revenge. The hurleystick comes down and catches the whore's ribs on the upswing.

The crowd is swelling in the tens. The prostitutes understand they are watching succession. This is what Helen wants. A story, a myth, a legend to build around the woman that now rules under the rebel statue. This is what the IRB does when they need to make examples of informers, traitors, and spies.

"Dear God." The beaten whore moans. Her cries for the supreme deity seem more heartfelt.

"Shut up. One good shot to your head and you're a resident at that Jewish hospital for nutters." Helen begins to transform back to human. That doesn't stop her from raising the stick, ready to use as logic demands. "Pack up and get lost. But I'm keeping the bell."

The defeated whore staggers to her feet. A trail of blood follows her across the stone terrace as she makes her exit.

"I'll get you. You bitch." She points a finger at Helen as if she is casting a curse, her words slurred. Her Dutch Boy haircut is matted by blood oozing from her ears. The light in her eyes dims.

Helen watches her adversary limp into the night. She holds the stick like a scepter and fixes her hat like a crown. The former statue whore stumbles across the street, her career at an end. She slumps against the streetlamp like a laboring ship against the rocks. She sinks to the curb. Shoes, purse, skirt, hairband, anything of value: everything will soon be picked clean from the wreckage by scavengers.

"Right, now. This is my corner of the park. Any fucking questions?" Helen carries her hurley stick like Excalibur. Her short speech is meant for the other women who practice the nocturnal art.

Helen's heart pounds. Euphoria takes her by the hand and waltzes her straight through the gates of depravity for hire.

16 The Morning After

Himself lies there, spread-eagled in all his glory, smelling like yesterday's trash. Helen has a troupe of step-dancers using her head as a dance floor. And that's the part of her that hurts the least. Her arms ache. Her legs throb. She doesn't want to think about why she hurts down there. She has no memory of what she did last night. Bits and pieces maybe, but she would never be able to make a story out of it. She remembers the hurleystick smashing into the whore's head. After that, she can't remember a thing.

It's afternoon and they're both still in bed. Aunt Margie barks at the kids. Young feet clomp-clomp around the cramped apartment.

"Any time Her Highness wants to get up." Aunt Margie doesn't factor Danny into the day.

"I'm up." Helen says it but she's still in bed looking at the ceiling. *What did you do? Helen asks herself as if she's speaking to another person. You did what? Unbelievable. For what?*

The "for what" question has an easy answer. There is a dollar bill along with a stack of coins on the dresser that weren't there yesterday or the day before that. What she did to earn those precious pieces of copper isn't so simple. She has no memory of faces. She has no memory of voices calling from the dark. That's the way Helen likes it. As close to not happening as it gets. But she still did it. How many times? In one night? Can't answer that. Look at the money on the dresser. That's the answer. *Do the calculations.*

Helen stumbles her way to the mirror above the washbasin. She can't look at herself. It's like staring into a carnival mirror. I came to America for this? I wish they caught me and hanged me. I'd be a heroine. Now what am I? *Alive, a voice answers in her head. Well, that's not good enough, she calls back.*

How do I hide this scar? Helen runs her finger along the wound. It's still fresh. Blood oozes from it. None of the johns cared about it. Helen hopes nobody saw it. The scarred whore has a notoriety that she wants to escape. The young girl from Donegal is gone forever. No time to mourn. Her replacement is already here.

Danny rises like a smelly Lazarus. He growls, he's hungry, he wants to vomit, his head hurts, he has to take a piss.

Helen ignores him. She goes to wash her hands clean in the basin. This must have been what Pilate went through. Attempts to wash off the stain of guilt are futile. The dirt and grime wash off, but the blood, the sin, remains. She puts a wet rag between her legs. The cold water stings. Christ, she aches. Helen pulls her nightshirt up. She's covered with black-and-blue fingermarks around her thighs and hips. She pulls the shirt's neckline down so she can see her shoulders. More fingermarks and bruises. None of it is tucked away in her memory. It's as if she was transported through time, direct from when the whore dropped to now.

"Helen, will you take these little ones from me?" Aunt Margie is holding the two boys like sacks of barley. Helen sits in front of the mirror, a broken soldier counting wounds. "Oh dear God."

Aunt Margie drops the boys. She walks over to Helen and puts an arm around her. They both start to cry.

"I should never have introduced you to that tart." Aunt Margie runs her fingers through Helen's hair. "It's her fault. She should have taken you to a shop or restaurant to get work."

Helen stops crying. She looks at Danny sprawled out on the bed, barely alive. Next to the bed is the dresser. The answer to all her problems sits on top.

"This isn't what I wanted. You know, it could be worse," Aunt Margie babbles. "You had a choice. There are other things to do in this world."

Helen covers her ears. She's looking for a specific pronoun, verb, or adjective that's not forthcoming. Aunt Margie is nothing more than an overacting performer in a silent melodrama. Helen walks over to the dresser and picks up the money. She holds it tight, weighs its value. Aunt Margie hovers around, lips flapping silently. Helen picks out fresh undergarments from the dresser. Her aunt's chest-clutching is getting annoying. Helen finishes getting dressed by placing her hat neatly on her head. She arranges the veil just so over her scar.

"Shut up." Helen turns to Aunt Margie. "Shut up and watch the boys. I'm going out."

Aunt Margie stands silent. This isn't the girl she took in two years ago.

"Danny. Danny!" Helen roars at her husband. "Get up!"

"What?" He emerges from his self-induced coma. He rubs his eyes and coughs up something evil from his lungs.

Stiff-legged and red-eyed, Danny staggers over to his wife. He looks her square in the eye. There's something about the missus that's different. He walks around her, inspecting her like meat hanging on a hook. He wags a finger like he's in on the joke.

"I see what it is." Danny has a smug look, but he might still be drunk from last night.

Helen is as cold as a statue. She's not going to put up with anyone's shit, and she's not going to tip her hand. Margie sees a battle brewing and runs for cover.

"Something's different with you," Danny stumbles in for a closer look, then stumbles back. "You're afraid to tell me. That's it. You don't want to tell me."

Helen stands stoic. She isn't going to say anything. Margie is sobbing in the other room changing nappies, waiting for the bombs to start falling.

"It's the …" Danny holds his words, waiting for Helen to flinch. "It's the fucking hat. It's new. You blew through our cash so you can get a fucking hat."

"Yes Danny, it's the hat. You're like a Royal Irish Constablulary copper. You caught me," Helen mocks him. "Out of my way. Take care of Bobby and Jack. Do what Margie says. I'll be back."

"Who are you to talk to me like that?" Danny strikes a tough-guy pose. It's hard to pull off when you weigh less than ten stone, your ribs show, you're wearing only undershorts and dirty socks.

"I'll talk to you as I please." The door slams. End of discussion.

Helen explodes from the apartment house and out onto Bonaparte Street. The sun hits her face and she feels good for a moment. She bounds down the street. The jingle in her pocket keeps time like a tambourine. She passes the shops and window displays, passes a thousand indulgences. Sunshine forces the coat off her as she marches up Lexington Street. Her pale white skin turns pink. It feels almost like heaven.

Helen storms the markets. There's an argument over the quality of fruit. No bruises today, buster. Fresh bread today, pal. None of the stale dry shit sold on the cheap. And get me a chicken for the pot. Her coat hangs off her arm while she juggles a couple of bags. The scent of apples and cinnamon cookies makes her sneeze. Today she is like anyone else. Her money is as good as anyone else's. It doesn't matter what she did to earn it. It was earned, not a handout, not charity. Hard, horrible, filthy work, *but tonight my kids eat well.*

Work is work, but there is a shame to what she does. That's why she keeps her head down and hides her trademark scar. Like every other whore since Magdalene, she feels the eyes of judgment on her. Those same eyes that seek her services at night point and call "harlot" by day. But the sun shines the same on everyone. Helen throws off those feelings. It always comes down to the cash. Today she has some.

Helen feels like an overpacked mule. She decides it's time to invest in a grocery cart. Another haul like this will surely break her back. She marches to the old tune *Rocky Road to Dublin playing in her mind. That song always makes her think about Danny dancing in the old days. Helen almost smiles.*

Hutzler's window displays are changing for the season. Helen stops and watches. She sets down the bags to give her arms a break. The workmen are striking the mock pier display. Helen watches with great interest. Her fingers press against the window. The two little sailors sit there as if there is somewhere to go. Damn, this better not be the last time those suits are for sale. She didn't earn enough last night to make a purchase. It was barely enough to get dinner for tonight.

Helen sees she has to think bigger. How many johns will it take to buy those sailor suits? Maybe Danny's union rantings make sense in this business. Perhaps in time Helen can get all the girls working together, setting rates, providing protection, sharing profits. Helen could be the booking agent for the girls. Dreams. When did being a prosperous whore become a dream?

17: October 5, 1918, 4:00 am: Baltimore

It's almost four in the morning and cold as hell dockside. Out in the dark, ship horns complain. Danny hangs around stomping on his feet to keep warm, hands in his pockets. His breath billows around his head like exhaust from a steam engine. He waits for trucks to show up that need unloading, usually produce from the Eastern Shore, bound for the Baltimore markets. Then they need to be reloaded with merchandise from the ships. At four bits a truck, Danny hopes to keep himself in whiskey and have a few coins extra. How much he makes depends on how many trucks, ships, and desperate men show up.

Danny stands in a queue with other drunks, addicts, and Coloreds all feeding at the bottom of the labor pond. Danny stands up straight to feel superior to the men in line. It's a chore with no real reward. He's still standing in line with his hand out just like everyone else. The drivers don't pick the help on a first-come, first-served basis—more likely the bigger backs and duller minds.

The truckers bark endlessly at the day laborers, while the union dockworkers threaten them for infringing on their territory. Danny doesn't give a shit. All he can think about is the sweet burn of whiskey going down his throat. After that nothing goes through his mind. In fact, his existence is dedicated to not having another thought. He chooses to be one of the walking dead. If he can't be drinking, he prefers to be unconscious. All Danny can think about is that day. That picnic. He had been hoping to kiss Helen for the first time that day. He drinks to not think about not thinking about that day.

A burly foreman in a seaman's cap and pea coat walks the line of men, picking out the best of the litter. There aren't that many trucks, so he can be choosy. He selects four men quickly and has them running down to the truck bays. The remaining men try to look strong, but miles of wear and tear, gallons of booze, and kilos of opium make that a tough act.

"You and you." The foreman points to Danny and the man next to him.

Danny looks over, and then up, to see that man's face. Towering over him is a Colored. In the old country, Danny never saw one, at least not up close.

They could be seen in the big harbor towns around the docks, usually sailors or working the ships as cooks or waiters; but in the country, never. Now, Danny is thrown in with the same lot.

"Sir, your lordship," Danny walks up to the burly man. "You think you could pair me up with someone else, eh?"

Danny looks at the colored man. He's a big man, strong as a beast.

"What?" The burly foreman is pissed. "I picked him first. You can go home."

"Thank you, your lordship, this will do fine." Danny submits and meekly looks at his new partner.

"You two get the last four trucks lined up in bay eight."

Hands in coat pockets, trying to stay warm, Danny trots down to the truck bays. The Colored walks deliberately behind, steam pouring off his shaved head, wearing a flannel shirt with sleeves torn off to accommodate his shoulders and biceps.

The first truck doors open. It's stacked to the ceiling with produce, the last for the season, from the Eastern Shore. It seems like an endless chore. Danny moves slowly, stacking his hand truck at a glacial pace. The Colored gets right to it with a hand truck and starts unloading. Quickly, the load disappears.

The first truck is dispatched. The next one rolls in, doors open, and the process repeats.

"Do you think you might help with this one?" The Colored has a deep voice. He doesn't sound like a city person.

"What? You need to speak up."

"I said, do you think you might help with this one." The colored man's voice booms throughout the loading dock.

"I'm moving at the speed God intended. No need to shout."

126

"Don't blaspheme the Lord. You're just another lazy white boy trying to take away my living." The Colored gives Danny a stern look.

Danny doesn't know what to say, so he starts loading his hand truck. It's tedious work, time moves slowly, and Danny likes to talk. He changes the subject to something he thinks he knows about: himself.

"I barely remember me old self. The one that wrote poems and sang with great heart. The old self that had dreams of seeing the world and being a great writer in grand Irish tradition. That was all before 'that Eastertide in the springtime of the year.'" Danny slams a crate on the ground thinking about it.

"Tom," the Colored says. "My name is Tom. Tom Willis. If you are going to be like every other white boy telling me why this work is beneath him, you should know my name."

"I'm Irish, nothing is beneath me." He offloads his hand truck and goes to fill it again. "You need to speak up. I'm a bit hard of hearing."

"Well, Irish, during the war, I heard all them white pilots. All full of themselves, flying above everyone. Not getting themselves bloody." Tom tosses a huge bag onto a hand truck. "But I don't fill the plane up with gas and tighten all them bolts, them pilots weren't going nowhere."

It's true Danny is just another white boy with a sad story, lumping trucks. With every crate and box, Danny drives his anger deeper into a pit. The loading and unloading work is a catharsis for Danny. His actions have a real effect. A crate needs to move; he puts his back to it, and it does. That day he had no effect. He was useless, pinned to that tree. It was like being a baby, helpless, caged in a crib, unable to understand what was happening. He was denied the chance to do the one thing he would have given his life for. As that thought creeps into his mind, he slams another crate onto a hand truck and shoves it to the loading dock.

"I like the English," Tom says to break the silence. "I was there during the war. Found you-all very polite."

"I'm Irish." Danny shoves a crate along the floor. "Can't say I share the same experience."

"All the same to me." Tom has stepped into a wasp's nest.

Danny stops shoving crates.

"It's not the same thing. One's the master, the other is the servant." Danny feels a fire lit inside him. "One is an oppressor, and the other is the oppressed. One's the hammer, the other the nail. One's a butcher, the other the butchered."

"You both look the same to me. Talk funny, pale, full of yourselves, blind to everything around you."

"We're treated like niggers in our own country. Do you have any idea what that's like? I mean in the land of our ancestors." Danny slams a crate of lettuce.

"You think I don't know what you mean?" Tom rolls his eyes. "My family Bible goes back about two hundred years in Talbot County. This is more my country than most white boys. I seen folk dragged out of bed in the middle of the night. Strung up by a mob, police watching every move. Don't eat here, don't drink there, white piss only. Yeah, I know what it's like to be a nigger in my own country."

Danny stops for a long, thoughtful moment. Throw in some spies, traitors, and a few martyrs—Tom Willis could be Irish.

"Nobody is a nigger or a paddy unless they believe themselves to be." Danny grabs Tom by the shoulder. Shit, if Danny could be sober two days in a row, he'd sound like an IRB recruiter. "There may be an ocean between us, but you and me are here on the bottom trying to find some justice. It's up to us to change things. We are the revolution."

Tom Willis looks at this strange white boy. Danny feels the kindled fire swell.

"My people are strewn all over the world. They stole our land, stole our dignity, stole our language, starved us, made us prison labor, shipped us off like freight to places nobody ever heard of on the other side of the world." Danny sounds like a big-tent preacher.

Tom Willis can't believe what he's hearing.

"Save your talk of the revolution for the sweatshops and slaughterhouses." Tom stops what he's doing and looks around. "Your revolution is finished right here, in these trucks and on these docks. We're all equal here. Everyone's hand is out looking for food. White, colored, spic or chink, if you're in this line you are equal to the man next to you. It doesn't matter where you came from or what you did. Nobody cares. Whatever happened on that little island of yours, nobody cares. Here, all that matters is now and what are you going to eat tomorrow.

"At the end of your revolution"—Tom Willis looks Danny straight in the eyes for a thoughtful second—"When your revolution is over, I'll still be a black man in your world."

That shut Danny up.

A strange ballet of motion performs in the early morning chill. It's as physical as it is mind-numbing, but Danny and Tom find a way to work together. A head nod, a point of the finger, a timed grunt, and the last of the trucks is unloaded in mutually agreed-upon silence. The two men form a bond the dwellers of the bottom strata sometimes make. They bear a common cross beyond oceans and race.

By seven in the morning, the work for the day is done. Morning clouds are just starting to give in to the sun. The trucks are rolling out to Washington and up to Harrisburg. Still tied to the piers, the ships wait on the tide. A trucker walks around and puts two bucks in each man's hand. Danny takes his pay. He crushes the cash in his hand with pressure enough to turn coal to diamonds.

Danny starts his trek toward the nearest saloon. He finds himself on the same path as Tom Willis.

"You're a fine man, Tom. How about you and me have a drink?" Danny slaps his new friend on the back.

"Thanks." Tom Willis keeps his straitlaced demeanor.

They walk in silence for a few blocks. It's a comfortable silence, but Danny needs to burst into a chorus of words. All that is required is a little lubrication.

The bar's sign, Gandy Dancer, buzzes like an angry hornet's nest. Danny starts toward the door, expecting his new friend to follow.

"This is where I keep moving." Tom taps Danny on the shoulder.

"Why? We're ahead of the crowd. I know the barkeep, he'll take care of us." Danny is surprised anyone would pass on an opportunity to drink.

"Irish, I'm a Baptist, and we don't drink, and I don't think my grandmama would be happy if I went into a place that serves liquor." This is beyond what Danny can comprehend.

"Ahh, have some Coca-Cola or seltzer." Danny scratches his head.

"It's not just that. There's another problem."

Danny stops with the door handle in his hand. "Fuck, you're a Protestant. Sorry mate. I didn't think."

"That doesn't matter." Tom shakes his head, wondering what world this Irishman is from. "I'm colored, I'm not welcome."

"Jesus."

"This is where we part ways." Tom shakes Danny's hand.

"Hey Irish, I hope I don't see you again at the docks. But—maybe I see you again." Tom Willis takes the path that leads home with some money in his pocket. Danny chooses the other.

18: October 5, 1918, 7:25 am: Gandy Dancer Saloon

The Gandy Dancer's sign sparks as a blaspheming muezzin calling the faithful, like Danny, to his morning rites. He skips through the door in anticipation. He slams his coin on the bar.

"De dhíth orm deoch." Danny says he needs a drink.

The barkeep is from the old country and doesn't look up at the request. He returns with a shot and some change. Danny caresses the shot glass for a moment, like foreplay. He brings it up to eye level at a ceremonial pace. Right now he is as happy as he gets. The anticipation of sweet release is exquisite. The golden elixir catches the morning light and outshines his memories. He smacks his lips and downs the drink in a gulp. The bad memories are flushed down into his personal drainage ditch.

Here's where all Danny's problems churn. His gut is with lined warrants posted by the Crown. Images of Helen's violation flash like lightning bolts striking his heart. Then the endless cries of hungry babies: nails in the cross. He hunts for work to shut them up, but it's the same story. *There are too many lads back from the war who need work. Where are you from? You Irish carry disease. The flu killing us is your fault. We hire Americans first.* Bills pile up, the wife barely speaks to him; just as well, he has no answers. The Devil and King Edward brought this misery to him. Now he is a ghost living in a strange country. If he goes home back to the old sod, he's a dead man. There are a few things the Crown can be counted on, not forgetting and not forgiving. In this new country, he is just another drunk poet who can't shit a word out of his ass. Danny kicks the barstool next to him. What's the fucking use?

"Another." Danny doesn't make eye contact with the barkeep. He slides a coin toward the man. The whiskey is a wild, unruly mistress. A man pays the price but the bliss she brings makes him sing. The whiskey knows him like no one can and goes straight to where he hurts.

He eyes the whiskey like a girl he's about to kiss. The morning light reflects off its silken amber surface, free of blemish or fault. Perfection created in a wooden cask. Unlike the first drink, he savors this one. He lets his fingers roam around the rim of the glass. He tastes the liquor off his fingertip. The smell of barley finds his nose, and he exults in its aroma. When expectation can no longer be harnessed, he downs the shot in a hungry instant.

The beautiful distillation works its magic. It transports Danny into back to the dreadful day in the spring of 1916. It promises a new and different memory for him as soon as he buys another drink.

"Barkeep." Danny holds up the empty shotglass.

"Christ, man. Have something to eat first." The barkeep tries to keep his countryman on the strait and narrow, not a natural preoccupation.

"Fuck all. I'll have another." Danny's mind drifts back to that day. This time he's armed with enough whiskey to change history.

Danny holds the drink in his hand. The whiskey is a cunt playing with his heart. This time the amber slut reveals nothing he wants to see. The shot glass mocks him. He looks in the mirror behind the bar and sees just a drunk trying to find a reason, an excuse for everything that's gone wrong. Bitch.

"One more," Danny demands, griping the shot-glass like a hand around a throat. He reminds the whiskey she's a hired whore, here to serve his pleasure. He tosses his head back, downs the drink, and is transported to Donegal.

This time the whiskey helps Danny free himself from the shackles that bound him to that tree. This time the whiskey allows Danny to fight like an ax-wielding Cú Chulainn and take down the slow-witted English sergeant. This time Danny rallies the two Irishmen to subdue the two English soldiers. This time Danny is the hero. This time Helen gives him the hero's kiss.

"Another." Danny slurs his demand.

"You're out of cash mate, time to take it home." The barkeep throws a bar rag over his shoulder and takes the empty glass from Danny.

"Ah, fuck." Danny stands up, a little wobbly. He starts for the door. He'll have to tell Helen there weren't any trucks this morning. She won't be happy. But the hell with her. Maybe she should get a job instead of spending her night volunteering with those temperance women.

"Christ, it's cold." Danny stumbles into the morning and turns his collar up against the weather.

19: October 10, 1919, 1:35 am: Aunt Margie's apartment

It's late at night. Helen is out with the temperance women again, Margie and Frank are at the pub, it's a sure bet.

Danny falls asleep on the small writing table and wakes to find drool from his mouth soaking the paper. Eyes unfocused, he makes out the outline of the whiskey bottle. His instinct is to grab it like his life depends on it. He takes an uncoordinated swipe at the bottle and knocks over an unseen shot-glass. The sound of breaking glass wakes the twins.

"Ah fuck." Barefoot, Danny tries to walk around the broken glass but doesn't see one stray piece.

"Jesus," Danny howls.

His foot has a nice gash in it along the sole. Danny looks to see if there is any whiskey left. There's maybe a shot left. He has a tough choice to make. Drink it or pour it on the wound.

"Fuck," Danny groans, accompanied by a chorus of crying angry kids.

Danny carefully grabs the bottle and swallows the last few drops. His foot stings enough to bring a tear to his eyes. The twins have awakened, startled by the sudden noise. Danny drags himself over to the bed they share and tries to calm the twins down. He'll do anything to shut them up.

"Shhh, shhh. Come on, you little beggars, it's all right. Everything is grand. Shhhh." Danny scoops up one and then the other and bounces them off his hips. He hobbles back and forth across the living room.

"There we go, lads. Feel free to suck your thumb. I did till I was twelve. Don't tell anyone." He looks over at the whiskey bottle. The residue of its contents clings to the insides and drips to the bottom. "That's it. Stuff your gob with the thumbs. There we go, you little bastards."

In his arms are two little creatures who look at him with complete trust. Their little arms cling around his neck, and their monkey legs embrace him.

Danny limps over to the worn-out paisley couch and crashes onto with the kids.

"My foot hurts like a son of a bitch. Don't repeat that. Do you even talk?" Danny looks at the twins as if they are strangers he's just met.

"I'm sorry, but which one is which?" Danny doesn't feel that bad not knowing who is who. They're not his kids. He'd watch Helen play with them. There's a strange bond beyond just mother and children. They are survivors of a horrific moment, bonded by experience as well as blood. It looks like a shared secret language between the three of them. A language he'll never learn. They look at him as if he is something other. Something other than what made them. He will always be an outsider looking in. Danny knows full well who made them. The Devil conceived them. He gets to take care of them.

"The one called Jack, raise your hand." Danny should have known. They both raise their hands. "All right. Bob, raise your hand. Just Bob, right."

The outcome is predictable. The two boys think it's funny.

"Come on, that's not fair." Danny feels the weight of innocent eyes bearing down on him. No expectations, no judgments, no conditions, just the eyes of children asking for affection. "Hold that till the mother gets home."

"You know this wasn't my idea." Danny waves at everything around him. "I didn't want this. But I couldn't do anything about it."

The twins crawl around the couch. Danny keeps them contained until he can clean up the glass.

20: October 19, 1919: Danny finds out

"Lovely, himself rises, and it's not even dinnertime." Margie looks at Danny still lying in a squalid bed dressed in yesterday's clothes. "Christ, you stink like a condemned brewery."

"Agh, I might have had a few too many pints last night." Danny sits up, stroking his head around the temples. The afternoon light crashes through the window like an interrogator's light demanding the truth. His feet reach the floor uncertainly.

"That's grand. Let's print that in the headlines—Danny Mc ..." Margie is interrupted by the boys crying. "Dammit. I'm not the nanny. You need to get up and take care of your kids."

"My kids," Danny snorts without thinking. "If you only knew."

"Knew what?" Margie gives Danny a stern look. She has always thought there was something about Danny and the twins that wasn't right. "Knew what?"

"Ah, it's nothing." Danny waves the woman off.

"Bullshit. I know there is more to what you told me." Margie is a big woman and imposes her girth on Danny, trapping him between her and the bed frame. "Now out with it."

"Please leave it be." Danny climbs up on the bed trying to escape her.

"No. You tell me the truth. I deserve it. You've been here over two years. Two years of watching you lay about drunk, your kids crying and shitting. Your wife, always wingeing and hell if you knew what she was up to—you'd have a fit beyond your wildest nightmare," Margie yells.

As the words come tumbling out, Margie holds her hand in front of her mouth. She hopes they can each keep their secret and forget this conversation ever happened.

"I'll take care of the twins. You go clean up." Margie puts her head down and quietly retreats to the kitchen.

"Not so fast. What do you mean? What's Helen up to?" Danny reaches out and grabs Margie by the shoulder. "She's my wife."

"Then act like a husband." Margie pulls away and walks toward the window. Her eyes want to look at anything that's not Danny or the twins. There's a coal delivery across the street that attracts her attention.

"Tell me what my wife is up to." Danny's blood curdles like milk gone bad. He's sweating out the toxins and raw emotion. He makes a fist, not sure who it's meant for, but someone deserves to be punched.

"Go look in the icebox. Then go ask yourself where all that food comes from." Margie is still looking out the window, trying to find the right words.

"I know, it's from Helen working for the temperance people. She told me she is a secretary. And whatever I bring in from loading trucks." Danny rights himself, trying to find solid footing.

"What you bring in?" Margie laughs and turns to face Danny. "What kind of secretary goes to work after sunset? You can't be this stupid?"

Margie points to the boys' wardrobe. "Go look in there. Are those the dandy clothes a temperance worker can afford to buy her kids?"

Margie points to Helen's wardrobe. "Are those the clothes temperance secretaries wear to work?"

Danny rips open the doors to the wardrobe. Tears start trickling down his face. Confusion collides with his hangover. He goes through Helen's clothes. Thin, skimpy lace dresses, nothing a proper woman would wear beyond her bedroom.

"Have you seen her face? Do you think that's what you get working in an office?" Margie mimics a scar going from ear to jaw.

Danny shakes his head. He was always afraid to ask where it came from. The answer was guaranteed to be something he didn't want to hear.

"If you weren't passed out drunk, you would know your wife doesn't make it home 'til long after midnight. Where do you think she is?"

"Tell me 'if I knew what' and I'll tell you where this comes from." Margie pulls a leather pouch from behind the mirror by the front door. She shows the wrinkled dollar bills to Danny, then returns the pouch back to the mirror.

"Now tell me, if I only knew what?" Margie approaches Danny and corners him.

The apartment door opens, to the excitement of Jack and Bobby. Danny looks at Margie, then over at Helen making an entrance.

"Momma, momma," the boys yell, as excited as puppies.

Helen walks in with a bag full of groceries. The room has the thick air of heavy drama taking place without her.

"What's all this?" Helen hugs the boys while the groceries fall to the floor.

Margie backs away from Danny, trying to act casual.

"Oh, nothing. We were just talking." Margie heads to the kitchen. Surely there must be a chore that needs attending.

"You two were talking?" She stoops down to pick up the food on the floor. "Can you help mommy?"

The boys try to help. But it turns into monkey play.

"The two of you never talk. It must have been quite a chat."

"It was." Danny regains his composure. The battle between his head and stomach could change that. "Is that a new coat? Where did you get it?"

Helen is taking off her coat and hanging it on a hook by the door.

"Oh, this old thing. It's from Hutzler's department store. My boss's wife, she gave it to me when she got a new one." Helen doesn't look at Danny.

"The clothes in the boys' wardrobe, lovely, where are they from?" Danny turns sideways to Helen, ready to spar. He tries to find the chink in her armor.

"Same place. I have a very generous employer. Those clothes are for the holidays." Helen slides past Danny. "Can I help you in the kitchen, Aunt Margie?"

"No thank you."

"That's all right, I'll help anyway."

Tonight, Danny, Helen, Margie, and the boys sit around the dinner table with all the levity of the Last Supper. A bare lightbulb hangs over the table, casting a harsh light. Silence is broken by Jack and Bobby fooling around, playing with their food.

"Stop that." Helen smacks Bobby in the back of the head. "Manners at the table, young man. Jack, I don't want to have to talk to you too."

Bobby plays with his spaghetti and grins at his mother.

Danny stares at Helen, trying to imagine what she does at night without wanting to find the truth.

"Where's Uncle Frank?" Helen asks, hoping it's a neutral question.

"He probably lost and missed the trolley from Old Hilltop. If he won, he'd have taken a taxicab to show off." Margie has her own baggage on the cart.

"He loves the ponies, he does," Danny adds while spinning his pasta.

"It would be better if he loved the ones that win," Margie frowns.

Danny turns the other cheek and views Helen differently. He suddenly questions everything. Love, loyalty, the last of his dignity—shattered. He needs to understand his reality.

"Are you working tonight?" Danny asks Helen, without looking at her.

"Yes," Helen responds quietly, looking away.

"What's the name of your boss again?" Danny asks, trying to set a trap.

Helen plays with her food. She gets up with her plate.

Danny watches Helen vanish into the small kitchen. He closes his eyes, still trying to grasp his worst fears. "Sit and talk with us."

"Smith. It's Jim Smith. He's the regional director." Helen answers while cleaning off her plate. What a stupid name. She's disappointed she couldn't make up something better.

Danny just stares at her. Watching every nuance in her movement, he prays he's wrong. But he has to know. Where does she go? What does she do? *God, God, how much more can you throw on me?*

"Where has your friend, what's her name—Mary—been?" Danny stirs the pot.

"She's been sick." With syphilis, Helen thinks, but she isn't sure.

"I used to think she was in the opera or the circus." Danny is about to drop a big potato into the pot. "Now I think she looks a bit whorish."

Helen almost chokes.

Margie watches Danny and Helen. For young people, they're like an old couple with baggage ready to burst. A hurried marriage, trouble in the old country, and nobody wants to talk about it. The silence screams. Her eyes dart back and forth, waiting for one of them to crack. Danny is a drink away from spilling the truth. Helen will carry her charade to the grave if she has to. Margie knows herself. The worst part is holding onto Helen's secret. She's ready to sound that trumpet from the ramparts.

Helen silently washes dishes in the kitchen. The boys play peek-a-boo between her legs. Why is Danny suddenly asking so many questions? She prays Margie didn't say too much.

Danny gets up and breaks into Uncle Frank's cache of whiskey. He slings the bottle onto the table and orders Jack to get a glass.

"Good, now fuck off."

Jack nods his little head, turns, and runs smack into Bobby. They tumble over and can't decide whether to cry or laugh. Feeling a lack of interest from the adults, they get up and go about the business of being toddlers.

"Agh, that's the last I'll see of them tonight," Danny mutters.

Helen hides in the bedroom. She leans against the door and locks it. There's a flask of gin in her oversized bag. With a big swig and a shake of her head, Helen prepares herself. She looks in the mirror and hates what she sees. It's not just the scar along her jaw. It's the lines and bags under her eyes, carved from stress and secrets. Helen is barely twenty, looks forty, and feels eighty. She sees the bruises on her arms and shoulders, handprints from desperate johns. It was only a few years ago her long black hair flowed like a river of silk. Today, trimmed shorter, it's a perpetual tangle, coarse like a horse's tail. She sprays some toilet water around herself. It's more to kill the scent of the strangers that will fuck her tonight than to entice them. In silence, she starts to apply some makeup. She paves over the lines under her eyes. The bright red lipstick displays like a sideshow sign saying, "Put Your Cock Here." She unfolds her cotton stockings over her legs. They used to be muscular dancer's legs that spun her across the floor free and easy. Now they are just thick. Workhorse flanks to be driven by strange, faceless, silent men. The skimpy chemise slides over her head and shoulders. It free-falls to her knees, pausing at her hips. She wiggles the thin fabric into place.

She takes an ice pick from her bag and tucks it into her high-laced boot against her shin. It's a snug fit that gives her both a limp and confidence. The shoes have a tall heel that add a few inches to her stature and gives her ass an extra lift. It's murder on the toes, but these are the tools of the trade. She puts her warm wool coat on over the chemise so Danny doesn't see her work clothes. She gives herself another look in the mirror. Her hair is still a mess. She gives it a few perfunctory brushes but decides it's a lost cause. Fuck it. Nobody will be looking at her hair. All they want is what she offers between her legs. She's got boys to feed. It's time for work.

Jack and Bobby are asleep, and Margie is complaining about Frank. The horses haven't been kind, and neither are the bookies he owes money to, so he hasn't been home. Win or lose, it's the same with this fellow. Danny doesn't give a shit. He has his own cross to bear. He's got to know the truth, no matter how much it will hurt.

The statue of General Lee rides above the shrubs. His sword is raised high, like a call to dereliction. The park has a smell about it that conflicts with nature. Strong perfumes, tobacco, booze, and furtive sex extinguish the scent of the boxwood hedges. Bird sounds are replaced with the echo of whispers and secret needs.

Danny sees a small lantern fighting off the night at the statue's feet. Ghostlike, Helen moves between shadows and moonlight. Danny hides in the shrubbery and watches. It's not long before he sees what he came to see. His heart and stomach are about meet, as one breaks and the other drops.

A well-dressed man, slender, with a walking cane at his side and a bowler on his head, approaches Helen. He looks like a fine fellow who needs a diversion before he heads up Calvert Street to the wife and children. The man walks to the statue. Danny can see Helen turn her back to the man and raise her hand with one finger pointing toward the stars. He can't hear exactly what she is saying, catching only the stray syllable. The man walks silently over to the bench and rings the dinner bell twice.

Even though it's a cold night, Helen sheds her coat and reveals herself and her costume. The man walks over to Helen and opens his overcoat. They drift back into the General's shadow. Danny struggles with what his eyes see and his heart refuses. The man's voice gets loud, and he shoves Helen to the ground. She bounces up like a prizefighter. The words blur together, but it's clear the conversation isn't pleasant.

The man is no gentleman. He gives Helen a boxing combination that lands two punches to the eyes. Helen staggers and falls to the ground. Danny fights off the memories to stay in the present. He starts to move toward the battle. His eyes are planted on Helen.

Helen climbs to her knees. She never looks up at the man. Instead, she searches the ground for her hat. Calmly, she places it back on her head.

The man steps closer, fist raised. Helen grabs him by the balls and pulls him down to his knees. Danny realizes his wife is a much tougher than the tomboy hurling-player of long ago. She's a dangerous lioness.

Helen pulls out her ice pick. She places it on the man's throat, close enough for his pounding jugular vein to feel its point with each heartbeat. All the while, she squeezes his testicles like an olive press. Helen talks into the man's ear. The man shrinks as she applies pressure to his balls. He nods his head. It seems he has just found out what true submission feels like. He struggles to get his billfold from inside his coat. He opens it up and lets all the bills tumble out.

Helen releases the man as he slumps to the ground, curled up in a ball. Helen gives him a swift kick with the tip of her shoe, a clean shot under the ribs. The man holds up his hands in full surrender. He picks up the cash and delivers it to Helen like a vassal serving the queen. Helen holds the ice pick like a scepter, the tool's business end pointed at the man's throat. She takes a step in his direction, and he is off as fast as his legs will carry him.

The man is in full flight. He doesn't see Danny standing on the path. Danny looks back at the statue and can see Helen counting money in the moonlight. The man is a block away under a streetlamp, bent over, trying to catch his breath.

Danny walks up to the man; the "gentleman" is as well-dressed as any man you're going to find. Danny would hate him regardless. The man is leaning between the lamppost and his cane. He acts as if air is a hard commodity to come by.

"Rough night, eh?" Danny asks.

"What?" The man looks up, breathing hard, wondering who this peasant is.

Danny kicks the cane away. The man falls to the ground, his fine suit sullied. Danny picks up the cane and swings it against the lamppost. It shatters into pieces. Still holding the handle of the cane, Danny thinks about driving it into this fucking man's chest.

"Who are you?" The man is stunned.

Maybe it's an angel who whispers in his ear. Danny throws the cane out into the street, grabs the man by his collar.

"What were you fighting about?" Danny demands.

"Who?"

"That woman in the park. I saw you!" Danny isn't about to play games. He cocks his fist like he's ready to pull the trigger.

"She wanted too much money for her service." The man holds his hands up in front of his face.

"So you hit her. What about negotiation? I'm sure you're familiar with that." Danny shakes the man.

"She's just a whore. What is there to negotiate?"

"She's my fucking wife." Danny backhands the man with all his strength. "What else? What did she say?"

"She is a madwoman," the man cries. "She has a rule or something about talking. She said I broke the rule. Since when do bloody whores have rules?"

Danny gives him another backhand.

"Jesus, you're hurting me." The man curls up in defense.

"What else?" Danny is ready to strike again.

"She wanted to know the strangest thing," the man says.

"What was it? Come on, I'm about to kill you."

"She said, 'Tell me what I want to hear.' I didn't know what to say." The man has a plea for mercy in his eyes. "So I said, 'I'm sorry.' I emptied my wallet. There might have been a few hundred dollars in there."

Danny drops the man. Maybe it's the Devil, perhaps it's an angel on his shoulder, but one of them has a plan that seems to make sense.

21: October 20, 1919: Danny's night out

It's evening, and the October sun drops under the horizon. The wind blows cold. The smell of working fireplaces is in the air. The Gandy Dancer's door is open for business.

"A pint and the hair of the dog," Danny orders. He's only been up a few hours and still shakes from last night's drunk.

"Ah, you're good drinking mates." Danny addresses some bar-side companions. "You talk gibberish, but you're good listeners." Danny gives them a nod with his shot and throws it back. "That's for the nerves. This is suckling on the teat of my dark mother." He slurps the caramel head off a pint of stout.

"You know none of this was part of the plan. I had big dreams. Then you know what happened. I don't have to tell you. I'd like to say the worst part was not being able to do anything. But it wasn't. It was watching her give that dead lad a kiss. That should have been me telling that bastard to fuck off. That should have been me lying there dead." Danny works his pint. The bar mirror reflects an ugly truth. Out of defiance, Danny stares back at himself.

"You boys want another drink? Ah, of course, you do." Danny can be a good host with a few drinks in his belly and some jingle in his pocket. . Tonight's drinks are sponsored by pilfering Helen's rainy-day fund. He was surprised to see how much was stashed behind the mirror. The Devil is a good provider. So he felt no remorse grabbing a handful of cash for him and his pals.

"You should know the truth. After all was said and done, we had to leave home, and we had no chance to be picky about where we went and who we ran with. Tinkers, IRB, fishermen, thugs, you name it, we needed them to stay alive. You'd never believe it, but she was a sight to see. Oh, she shot that soldier boy and something changed. I give her that." Danny downs another shot.

"We didn't have nowhere to go, so we went where nobody goes. It was with that Tinker woman things started spinning out of control. We told her what happened and she understood. The old lady took us to her camp, and they took us in. Fed us and housed us. The Brits were no friends of the Tinkers. But I was nervous. Casting your trust to a pack of thieves is a risky business. Never mind running with the IRB. They had enough of their own problems. Everyone hated the Crown.

"It wasn't long before we figured her to be you know…. Why did we have to pay for someone else's crime? She didn't do anything wrong. What did I do? The idea of having that little runt running around made me sick. A constant reminder… It would be like looking at the Devil every fucking day.

"That's when the old lady offered us a way out. Oh sure, Helen said it wasn't the baby's fault either. But I didn't care. I'd always see those bastards' faces in their eyes. We argued for days about it. We were fugitives, for Christ's sake. We were going to be hanged if they caught us. We needed to leave Ireland and having a baby bulging in the belly wouldn't make it easy. I said we can start over—fresh. Oh, Jesus, I don't have to tell you that didn't make things better.

Oh—she took a good swing at me with a horse whip. Caught me good around the leg. That's when the old lady said something that changed everything." Danny pauses and looks over his stout, then takes a healthy gulp. "I need another."

The Double R Dance Band plays *The Rocky Road to Dublin* at a danceable tempo. Danny has had enough stout to feel like he's in the old country. His feet tap out the rhythm, and within a few bars, he's step-dancing, hair flowing, arms down at his side. Eyes closed, smile wide, Danny bounces in time to the music. Each footstep reminds him of a joyful time, a time filled with dreams.

The bar has only a few customers, mostly old men from the old country, heads down, tending their pints, sitting along the wall like stations of the cross. Danny has no competition for the dance floor. The first chorus, Danny stomps out the rhythm with the band. The second chorus is a challenge, the band speeds up, and Danny's feet and legs fly with ease. By now all eyes are on Danny commanding the dance floor. The third chorus, the dancer dares the band to speed along with him. The old men clap to the rhythm. Danny's feet are like a riveter's hammer pounding out the time. The drummer begins to sweat, the box player grimaces, the fiddle player grunts in time. The fourth verse is like two trains careening toward the station. Horse hair flies off the fiddle player's bow, drumsticks shatter, hand claps turn to applause, and on the beat, the trains stop. Danny collapses in an exhausted heap. The band laughs at their daring. For the entertainment, the hat passes to buy a round for Danny.

A pint and a shot come his way.

"Thanks, don't forget these two." Danny points to his drinking buddies. The bartender nods and gives a disapproving look at the same time. "I know it's late."

Danny turns to his audience of St. Patrick's Day patriots and old-timers from the old sod. He raises his pint high. "Up the Republic."

"Up the Republic," a sparse chorus answers, glasses barely raised.

Danny continues talking to his drinking pals. He can see the bewilderment in their eyes. His storytelling is a bit scattered, but they enjoy his company.

Danny looks into the shot glass, always expecting some form of truth or solution will one day spill out. So far this hasn't worked as hoped. He just gets drunker, and the echo of his anger gets louder.

"The thing that changed everything was the stupid old bitch. If you can believe this…" Danny leans in like he's telling a secret. "We went to see the Tinker woman to take care of the messy business. When she said, 'Because of the situation you have two fathers and two babies. . . .' Shit, I couldn't let a quack like that slice up Helen. We didn't know it was twins. But the old woman did. She knew it was twins. We thought she was a charlatan. She wanted double the fee, but it was that knife. That ended it. My sweet Helen wasn't going to be carved like a pumpkin. It was my own stupid idea to keep the babies. I guess I loved her. But I was never going to accept them as mine. I said the Devil can feed them."

Danny works his stout, pausing to let the sweet brown elixir run through his body.

"I'll have another. Except make it a double whiskey and a stout, if you'd be so kind." Danny feels the drink making its way to his brain. His mood lightens as his head clears. He knows what he's going to do. He has figured out how to make the agony in his heart stop. It is simple. Just one short step. One, two, three, jump. But before all that, he wants to go out in grand style. He wants to get good and drunk, that feeling like the first time he got drunk. He wants the room spinning like a carousel. He wants everything to sound funny, one big joke. He wants to see life's comedy play out to its end. And he wants to enjoy it with his drinking pals.

"Feeling flush, eh?" The bartender gives Danny a cautious eye. Danny isn't the kind of customer who has plenty of cash to spend.

"Feel like a king." Danny tips his drink to the bartender. "And tonight I'll give you a tip you will remember. In fact, treat yourself on me and have a cigar."

Danny turns to his friends. Attired in fine-fitting sailor suits, the pair smile and laugh at Danny.

"You know when I was a wee lad, I told me Da I was going to be famous. I was going to be Ireland's greatest poet. I was going to write a great Hero's Cycle. But before you write about something, you should do something. I should have been the hero then, and I should be a hero now. But I'm a drunk who can't do much of anything. What can I do? I still think there is another poem in this rock." Danny bangs on his head. His tone gets somber. "But I can't find it. So! Get a job, you say. Sure, easy to say. What do I do? I pounded the pavement and searched my soul at the bottom of every bottle. Apparently, the local employers are prejudiced against men of accents. And drunks.

"You know, I still feel that belt around my neck. I hear those gunshots and see Helen standing there." Danny takes a long pause, looks down at his feet. When he looks up, he says, "She was smiling. Ahh fuck, what am I crying about? Those bastards would have shot us dead. I should be clicking my heels to be fucking alive.

"Drink up lads, I'm starting to feel legless. We still have some walking to do." Danny throws back the double whiskey and downs the pint. "Come on then—drink up."

Danny watches his pals drink painfully slow. His head starts rolling around. The moment of clarity vanishes, and he's roaring drunk.

"Fuck it, that's enough. Let me wipe the milk off your faces, and we're off." Danny takes a bar rag and cleans the milk mustaches off Jack and Bobby. He pulls them off their barstools. He presses a five-dollar note nice and flat, then leaves it on the bar.

They stumble outside, two little boys in sailor suits and a man drunk beyond the word. Tripping over the curb and knocking into trash cans is high entertainment for the two lads, but Danny gets furious.

"Shut up, you little bastards." Danny gains a limp. "We got to take a bit of a side trip."

The side trip isn't that far. No more than a few blocks, but it feels like crossing a chasm on a rickety bridge. They're getting close to the park, and the air is getting thin. Danny holds the boys' hands very tight, tight enough to get complaints.

"Shut up." Danny's brisk pace keeps the boys airborne every few steps as they hold on to his hands and arms.

They stop across the street from the park. Danny sees the statue of General Lee riding tall above the hedge. From out of the shadows, the painted women step into the moonlight looking for customers. A few spot him and give him a wave, encouraging him to bring the boys over as well. He walks over, but not because of them. Along the shrubs and hedges, he can hear and smell the illicit activities going on in the shadows. He wants to vomit but fights to keep it down.

"How much?" A voice from the dark asks. The glow from a cigarette lights up. For a moment the face of a bearded man in glasses and a hat appears, then vanishes like a phantom.

"What?" Danny is caught off guard.

"In the sailor suits, how much." A low-pitched voice, formless in the dark, asks again.

"You fucking piece of shit. I should kill you." Danny raises his fist and almost falls over.

Danny shuffles the boys along quickly. Perverse predators salivate, wondering what he's doing here with little boys if not working them. His flesh crawls.

They get to the entrance leading to the statue of General Lee. Danny stands there and can see Helen with her back turned, leaning against the statue. There is a man on the bench, and he rings the bell. Danny can't look anymore. His mind is made up. Tonight his problems end. He looks at Jack and Bobby and shakes his head. It's best for everyone that he decide for them.

Danny grabs the boys by the arms and hurries them away from this place. His head spins and his stomach is ready to explode. The sidewalk is like navigating in high seas. He trips against the curb and runs into a big fellow. Danny looks up and sees he's been caught by a man that makes him look like a child. The man is about thirty and has the working clothes of a Pigtown butcher. The smell of whiskey on him tells Danny they're kindred spirits.

"You think you might spare a swig for a man to get his bearings straight?" Danny asks, with hope in his heart.

The big man looks Danny over. They both stagger and sway in an unnatural counterpoint. There's a bottle of whiskey in the stranger's hands. The big man looks the small boys over, mystified.

"These two? Hell, they were conceived by the Devil himself. I take no credit for them." Danny puts a finger to his lips like he's sharing a confidence. "It's our last night together. So how about it brother, just a swig?"

The big stranger looks Danny over one more time. He takes a long drag from his cigarette and blows it in Danny's face. His bearlike paw swipes Danny to the ground. "Fuck off." He storms off into the night.

Danny staggers to his feet with the help of Jack and Bobby. "Come on, lads. We've still a few blocks to go."

"Shut up, you little bastards." Danny gains a limp. "We got to take a bit of a side trip."

The side trip isn't that far. No more than a few blocks, but it feels like crossing a chasm on a rickety bridge. They're getting close to the park, and the air is getting thin. Danny holds the boys' hands very tight, tight enough to get complaints.

"Shut up." Danny's brisk pace keeps the boys airborne every few steps as they hold on to his hands and arms.

They stop across the street from the park. Danny sees the statue of General Lee riding tall above the hedge. From out of the shadows, the painted women step into the moonlight looking for customers. A few spot him and give him a wave, encouraging him to bring the boys over as well. He walks over, but not because of them. Along the shrubs and hedges, he can hear and smell the illicit activities going on in the shadows. He wants to vomit but fights to keep it down.

"How much?" A voice from the dark asks. The glow from a cigarette lights up. For a moment the face of a bearded man in glasses and a hat appears, then vanishes like a phantom.

"What?" Danny is caught off guard.

"In the sailor suits, how much." A low-pitched voice, formless in the dark, asks again.

"You fucking piece of shit. I should kill you." Danny raises his fist and almost falls over.

Danny shuffles the boys along quickly. Perverse predators salivate, wondering what he's doing here with little boys if not working them. His flesh crawls.

They get to the entrance leading to the statue of General Lee. Danny stands there and can see Helen with her back turned, leaning against the statue. There is a man on the bench, and he rings the bell. Danny can't look anymore. His mind is made up. Tonight his problems end. He looks at Jack and Bobby and shakes his head. It's best for everyone that he decides for everyone.

Danny grabs the boys by the arms and hurries them away from this place. His head spins and his stomach is ready to explode. Walking on the sidewalk is like navigating in high seas. He trips against the curb and runs into a big fellow. Danny looks up and sees he's been caught by a man that makes him look like a child. The man is about thirty and has the working clothes of a Pigtown butcher. The smell of whiskey on him tells Danny they're kindred spirits.

"You think you might spare a swig for a man to get his bearings straight?" Danny asks, with hope in his heart.

The big man looks Danny over. They both stagger and sway in an unnatural counterpoint. There's a bottle of whiskey in the stranger's hands. The big man looks the small boys over and is mystified.

"These two? Hell, they were conceived by the Devil himself. I take no credit for them." Danny puts a finger to his lips like he's sharing a confidence. "It's our last night together. So how about it brother, just a swig?"

The big stranger looks Danny over one more time. He takes a long drag from his cigarette and blows it in Danny's face. His bearlike paw swipes Danny to the ground. "Fuck off." He storms off into the night.

Danny staggers to his feet with the help of Jack and Bobby. "Come on, lads. We've still a few blocks to go."

22: October 20, 1919: The butcher's demise, Baltimore

"What are yew looking at, auld mohn?" Helen looks up at the statue of General Robert E. Lee. "Don't be looking at me like that."

The General returns an empty stare.

"Look, ah dew what ah have to dew."

The prolonged vowels betray Helen's Gaelic tongue. She has tried to suppress her accent by talking through her nose to sound more American. It doesn't work. A thousand days on, she still sounds straight off the boat.

"I have two wee ones shitting in their nappies and a drunk, lazy, do-less husband."

Once the moon rises she owns this corner of the park, and no one dares challenge her claim. Helen goes about her nightly ritual. She folds her wool winter coat. Then she places a dinner bell on the park bench across from the General's statue. On the pedestal's corner, by the General's feet, she sets a kerosene lamp. The match head strikes granite, and the wick ignites. The General's statue lights up with an eerie glow battling the moonlight. If this were a church, she might genuflect, but she is as far from religion as she is from her old home.

"At least you know the rule. No talking. And I trust those dead eyes can't see. These other bastards have to be reminded." *General Robert E. Lee - Commander of the Army of the Confederate States of America.* Helen read the inscription at the stone figure's feet hundreds of times. She's long lost count. It's been a rough ten months. "You're not the first stone-dead rebel hero I've met. The old country is littered with your kind. Heroes of lost causes. Why we worship your kind as stone gods, it's beyond me. You are nothing more than another dead rebel—who lost. In a hundred years no one will know your name or care what you fought for."

Helen takes in a great breath and lets out a soft sigh. She gives herself a peaceful moment before she opens shop. Her mind plays like the silent films she adores. The projector beams sepia-colored memories of a slender young girl full of love and craic. The girl is adrift in a rowboat with her lover. Her head rests in his lap. She reaches up, letting her hands float in his waves of black hair. She loves that his eyes are the same color as a tormented sea. Whiskey whispers in his ear and poetry stumbles out his mouth. Each word sends young Helen into a dreamy world of hopes and dreams.

"Excuse me." A shy voice emerges from the shadows behind Helen.

"Shut up. There are two rules. One—I don't want to hear you, so don't talk. Two,"—with Helen's back to the stranger, she holds up two fingers for emphasis—"I don't want to see you." Helen stiffens her arms against the statue's pedestal. "If you understand, ring the bell behind you twice. Once if not."

Helen waits for the sound. Indecision, embodied in soft footsteps, walks over to the bench. There's a momentary silence. The bell rings twice.

"Good. I'll show you me wares. If you like what you see, ring twice. If not—ring once and walk away. And don't take all night—it's cold out." Helen stands in front of the kerosene lantern with her back to the lad. She adjusts the plume in her Alpine-style hat and spreads its veil across her face. The sheer satin chemise opens like an angel spreading its wings. The lamp's amber glow reveals Helen's motherly shape, rounded hips supported by stocky legs. The angel wings drop. With a vaudevillian flair, she lets the rose-patterned chemise fall slightly off the left shoulder, then the right, leaving her bare across the neck and shoulders on a cold autumn night. The young stranger's feet shuffle. Helen senses her power taking hold. With a dancer's grace, she bends over. She begins to pull up the well-worn hem of her chemise, revealing the stockings above her high-top, tall-heeled shoes. The lad starts heavy breathing. "Hold on. There's more."

Helen raises up her chemise like a theatre curtain opening to a private audience. Her cotton stockings stretch from her crumpled garters like well-worn spare skin. Where the stockings end, the star of the show appears.

Helen's presentation is somewhere between beauty contest and barnyard animal husbandry. She holds onto the pedestal and stares ahead to read *General Robert E. Lee*. Cool air grazes across her plump bottom, raising goosebumps.

The lad's pocket watch makes the silence thicker, each tick an eternity to its tock. Helen waits to find out if her ass strikes a stranger's fancy. The bell rings once. She can hear some breathing and her stranger say in near falsetto, "If you don't mind…" The bell rings again. Lowering to an alto's voice range, the lad tries again. "I'd like to…"

"Were your parents brother and sister? Are you a complete dunce? The first rule: Don't talk." Helen points to the lantern lighting up a pile of coins. "Start dropping coins till I tell you to stop." She senses someone new to this game, maybe even a virgin. She transmigrates herself into a she-wolf of Celtic lore. Time to feed.

Out of the corner of her eye, Helen sees a hand placing a coin next to the oil lamp.

"Try again." The hand is smooth and white, nails clean and neat. It's a hand of the sweet life. At the base of the pedestal, she can see the stranger's excellent patent leather wingtip shoes shining in the moonlight.

Another coin drops next to the lantern.

"I said—keep dropping coins until I tell you to stop." Helen's tolerance for stupidity has a short wick. "Are you deaf?"

"No, ma'am." Two more coins are fed to the kitty.

"You are a fucking eejit! There are only two rules. Shut the fuck up is rule number one! Add another," she points to the coins. "Because you're pissing me off. Then get on with it." Helen, the she-wolf, just had her bite of flesh.

Eyes shut, chemise up, she braces herself for an at-best awkward attempt by a young boy. The smell of whiskey tumbles off him, so now she knows where the courage came from. Once she feels his breath about to touch her shoulder, she says. "We're not in love. Anything else is extra." Helen raises one cautionary finger. "First rule. Now get on with it."

The lad's belt buckle comes undone. As his trousers fall, loose change clangs like a call to supper. Helen tries to receive him, but his penis stumbles around with all the grace of a drunken sailor on shore leave. After few misguided tries, he batters at her forbidden spot.

"Stop. I was wrong. There are three rules. That's number three. I didn't think I needed to even mention it." Helen looks up at General Lee like a grandfather. "So—do they teach you anything at that church of yours? Jesus, Mary, and Joseph. That's Old Testament sin—the worst kind. Look, I'm going to have to show you how it's done. If I touch it, it's two bits more."

"Yes, ma'am." Another two coins clink under the lantern.

"Sweet Mother Mary and for all that is holy on this earth, why can't you shut the fuck up!" Helen is convinced she is dealing with an idiot child who has wandered off. "Now pass it through my legs, and I'll get this over with."

Compliant, the lad passes his penis to Helen, who inserts it into herself without ceremony. "Now hold my hips with your hands and have at it."

The boy's attempt to please himself, never mind anyone else, is like Helen waltzing to Strauss and him parading to Sousa. Her eyes swing between the General's title to the cash next to the kerosene lantern. She pushes back, wiggles, and bounces; anything that might hasten the boy's release. To kill time, she drifts back to the silent film in her mind.

Her poet whispers tender words in her ear. He recites verse after verse of love. But it's always the whiskey spinning the muse and him nothing more than taking dictation.

With each inelegant thrust from the lad, Helen thinks how she much would have preferred to live in Belfast or Liverpool. She crossed the ocean to Baltimore with a price on her head and a bump in her belly. The hopes of happiness sailed away on another course as she left Ireland on a trawler. Her man's poetic charms mean nothing in America. She was left with a drunk who couldn't steer nor row, hoe nor bale. His gift of gab has no use at a factory. All that talk of a worker's revolution couldn't get him a sweeper's job. Now that the Kaiser has packed up shop, even the army has no use for him. Now that the Spanish Flu is waning, gravediggers are back at work. None of that stopped the whiskey from filling his head with nonsense and false grandeur.

Behind her, Helen senses the lad ready to finish his business. A sound in the bushes catches her attention.

"If you want to watch—sit on the bench and have a coin ready. If you want a turn—ring the bell twice. And shut up. No talking!" Helen gives out commands as if she were a schoolmistress organizing the playground. "Let the boy finish his business."

Cigarette smoke drifts past Helen's nose. It causes her eyes to water and makes her sneeze, which in turn makes her shiver head to toe and elicit a moan from the lad.

"Don't you start making noise." Helen puts her head down as she absorbs the impact of the lad's hips. At this stage of her career, the feeling of a penis inside her was like a finger poking her in the ear. What's the difference between her and a fishmonger or chambermaid? What of the trash-man or gravedigger? Isn't she performing a service? Isn't she doing what no one else would do otherwise? Nobody dreams of shoveling shit or sucking a cock for a living. Some things just need doing. Her job is to touch the untouchable. For a few pieces of copper, she plies a trade the same as anyone else. Better, she makes old men feel young and turns boys into men. Helen glances side to side. This is her domain, her shop, this wooded sanctuary at the foot of a dead stone soldier. She's the queen, ruler of all, a sole proprietor until she returns to the greater world of useless husbands, soul-devouring children, and a society that sees her as a scourge. Why should she be scorned and shunned because she gives some poor sod a moment's pleasure?

Looking through her legs, she sees the feet of the new stranger. Blood-soaked work boots and the frayed edge of a butcher's apron.

The new stranger has a deep baritone cough that resonates from what must be cathedral-size lungs. He draws hard on his cigarette, followed by another round of coughing. He approaches like a stalking lion drunk from the blood of slow prey. Helen hears the gravel crush under his weight. He takes a final drag from his cigarette. It glows its last as he flicks it aside. The butt lands with a hiss in a puddle.

158

The breathing behind Helen gets heavier and faster while the hip pounding slows. Overwhelmed by the confusion and intrusion, the lad loses his erection like a penny in a deep pocket.

Helen looks at General Lee, hoping he can tell her what's going on behind her. A ruffian polishes off a bottle of bottom shelf-whiskey and stumbles toward her. The bronze general remains tight-lipped.

"Shit," the man mumbles. With no smoke or drink to entertain himself, he figures it's time to bang a whore. His feet compensate for his drunken brain's inefficiency. His experience with bullies makes short work of a Guilford swell in the wrong part of the city. There's a brief scuffle before Helen feels the penis snatched from inside her. Helen turns to see the man lift the lad up by the scruff of his neck and toss him like a rag doll to the ground.

"He's done." The thug looks at Helen then turns toward the youth. "Your mother's calling. Find her! Get out of here." The lad runs off terrified, but with a tale to tell his Johns Hopkins friends. Looking back toward Helen, the man says, "Now me. And don't tell me to shut up."

"Look at me." The thug spins Helen around. After a full week of "yes sir, no sir," he's full of a working man's drunken rage. A full week of little men telling a big man his business. A full week of mind-numbing and muscle-aching work. He'd be as happy to beat her as fuck her. Before Helen can raise a finger to invoke her rules, he cuts her off with a raised fist. Compassion or curiosity, either way, the man decides against beating. He sees her in a reality the drunk understand. Each boozy ounce strips away the veneer of civility, like a magnifying glass burning away the bullshit to get to the naked truth.

"So is this why you don't want to see anyone." The thug pushes Helen into the moonlight. She fights to hold her head down, but the thug forces up her chin with a rude jerk, knocking her veiled hat off. "You don't want us—to see you.

"Who was the one who was always telling *you* to shut up? Was the husband tired of a whoring wife? Maybe it was a harpie or one of them darkies with a temper." Helen's black eyes don't surprise him. A good whore needs to know her place. The boxer's nose means she needed reminding of that place. The man staggers to a self-righteous stance.

"Let me guess about that scar. The husband didn't do that." He runs his finger along the wound that stretches from Helen's ear, down the jawline and to the edge of her chin. It tells the story. She slaps his hand away.

"You're a bitch that's never going to know her place." The man nods his head. He's got her number, or so he thinks.

"The black eyes maybe, but not the scar. The husband wants you pretty enough to work in a shop or for a rich Bolton Hill family. You'd scare the children and customers off. But there's money to be made here on the streets. Customers ain't so picky. It was a darkie—wasn't it? They don't know how to treat a white woman." The man leans in to steal a violent kiss. Helen fends him off with both fists to his chest.

She gets an eyeful of the bastard. He stands well over six feet, with the big arms of a butcher. A bloody white apron dangles inside his open wool coat. Bloody boots to match. Helen prays he's a butcher. His cap is pulled close to his dark, dead eyes. He reeks of whiskey and tobacco.

"What's the going price for scar-faced whore? I bet you've more stab wounds and bruises under that cheap bodice." He leans in, an eyelash away from Helen's face. He opens the front of her chemise and leers down at her breasts. "I bet there's a cigarette burn or two down there. Hard for a whore to trade damaged goods, I bet."

He grabs her around the back of the head and throat with one paw. He lifts her off the ground and holds her at eye level. Like magic, a barber's razor blade appears in the other paw.

"There's one rule. My rule. I say what I want, and I do what I want when I'm paying a fucking whore. You'll be lucky I don't take your little pot of gold over there. Biddy." He brings the blade close to her throat for dramatic effect. "So you better be a good ride. Biddy."

The big ape has his thumb on Helen's windpipe. Her vision blurs. Breathing is a struggle. Her feet float off the ground, hanging and twitching like fresh slaughter. Spinning overhead she sees General Lee, sword raised, commanding her to rise up against her oppressor. Her eyes try to focus on her attacker's face. Helen's movie plays again in her oxygen-deprived mind. The thug's menacing face transforms into a movie screen. Tonight's short feature stars a montage of faces from the fucking king to the soldiers that stole her dignity, to the endless stream of men here in the park satisfying their needs. Relentless ghosts, haunting her memories, challenging her to fight back. The last scene is a close-up of a stiletto blade glistening in the moonlight, slashing through the night air. The film gets caught in the projector's sprockets and flames out on the screen. Rage overcomes her need to breathe. Helen is still a she-wolf who will not be tamed by a man.

Helen goes limp in the thug's hand and lifts her right knee. The thug sees this as a sign of her submission. He drops his guard and blade to undo his trousers. Reaching into her high-top shoe, she slides out an ice pick. She can be a magician too. As his trousers tumble around his ankles, Helen strikes. A quick thrust to his abdomen. At first, the thug is more stunned than injured. He stares in disbelief at Helen and lets go of her throat. With air pumping into her lungs, Helen regains her strength and strikes again. Under the rib cage, then an additional turn upward into the lungs and heart. The man collapses near his blade. Now it's his vision fading. He reaches for the razor lying just out of reach.

"You bitch." It's a mumble.

Helen grabs her hurly stick; she always keeps it waiting at the base of the stony-eyed general and swipes the blade away, leaving him as vulnerable as a baby. Using the stick for leverage, she rolls the thug over on his back like a side of beef. It's Friday, payday, he's sure to have some jingle in his pockets. Looking him in the eye, she leans over him. Nose to nose.

Helen sees a man whose time is marked. Blood flows from his abdomen, running between the paving stones. His internal injuries already are bleeding into his lungs and gurgling out the mouth. He looks at Helen, pleading for mercy.

Fool, she thinks, he should be asking forgiveness. Funny how his eyes are the color of a tormented sea. Helen almost smiles. "Tell me what I want to hear."

Helen's attacker doesn't respond. The world around him grows more distant by the second.

"I said no talking and I didn't want to see you. You broke my rules." With the detachment of a professional and her full weight, Helen plunges the ice pick into his throat. Blood shoots up as if from a broken faucet, soiling her dress. "Look at this mess. You're paying for this. A week's wage should cover it."

Going through his pockets, Helen discovers this poser couldn't get through Pigtown without drinking his weight in the pubs. She glares down at her attacker. "You fucking bastard. You were going to stiff me."

She puts a finger to his lips.

"Shh. Not a word. In three days you'll be buried, and in four even your own mother won't be mourning yew." She lets her Gaelic accent linger. "Biddy—me arse."

"Help…" Blood spills out of the thug's mouth.

Dispassionate, Helen stands over him. "Look up at the moon. Not a cloud in the sky. Not a drop of rain. Even the angels won't shed a tear for you."

She would like to think she had no emotion dispatching a nameless butcher to his maker, but that would be a lie. This drunken bully is about to be crucified to pay for the sins of a multitude of named and unnamed bastards. Helen laughs to herself and looks up at General Lee as if he were in on the joke. She places her foot on the butt of the ice pick's handle and drives the point to the paving stones. Helen delivers swift mercy, but forgiveness is God's job.

Helen retrieves the dinner bell from the bench and puts her coat on, afraid of catching a cold. Looking up at General Lee, she says, "You understand."

General Lee looks down from his horse. The butcher lies on his back, arms extended as if he's on the cross, with his pants wrapped around his ankles. Blood and life escape him. Helen refuses to glance back at the body, rule number two. She gathers her coins and snuffs out the kerosene lantern.

162

"I said no talking."

23: October 21,1919: After midnight

The tide is turning around, and the harbor traffic goes to work under a clear night.

"Be good lads and see if you can carry two bricks each. That's it, lads. Bring them over here." Danny points to a stack of bricks meant to repair a wall at the sugar factory. The boys run about the task, trying to please.

"That's good, lads. I'll take them."

Danny has had his eye on an abandoned rowboat hung up under the wharf near the Domino Sugars factory. He didn't know what to do with it until this plan brewed in his brain. With luck, it's only rainwater at the bottom of the boat. He treats the bricks like precious cargo, then tosses the boys in like baggage. Their beautiful white sailor suits get wet and stained when they land on the seats. Danny pulls a knife from his pocket. Silently, he cuts the slimy, rotting rope clinging to the pylon. He uses a broken paddle to shove off.

Jack and Bobby sit on the front seat, nervous and shivering, clinging to each other. This is the first time they've ever been off dry land. Their young minds realize that the charming clown in the bar has changed his costume.

"Aye, you're real sailors now."

Danny rows the boat in silence. As they drift from the pier, waves from the wakes of the work boats increase. The boys grab the boat's sides for dear life as it rolls. Ship horns, whistles, bells, and shouts from deckhands blend together on the water. The farther away from the pier, the bigger the waves get. Danny, the captain, navigates his rowboat into the tempest.

"Funny, almost poetic. It all began in a rowboat almost like this with your mother." Danny's speech slurs. "Tonight it ends here. The final stanza.

"It's my fault. Maybe I should have let the Tinker woman fix things. Maybe I should never have told the Devil to take care of his own. I had no idea how he'd do it." Danny tears up. "With the two of you gone, she won't have to do what she does. Oh sure, she'll be wailing and mourning, but time will pass."

A big wave nearly tips the rowboat over.

"Hold on, lads. I guess it doesn't matter how far we go." Danny looks up and sees another wave on its way. "Here come some more."

A tug blasts its horn. Deckhands yell at Danny and his crew. The rowboat bounces at the whim of the wake. Danny puts his back to it and steers away from the piers and wharves.

"The Devil gave you life, he can take you back. I want my Helen back, the way it was. Shite, I know it can never be that way again. But I want her to myself—not share her with Satan's bastards."

Danny gets the rowboat into the middle of the harbor's narrow neck.

"Maybe God made you twins on purpose. One an angel and one a devil. Only how do I know which is which? Then it came to me." Danny points to his head. "It came like a lightning bolt. Let God show me. He will give me a sign. It's all his grand fucking design, isn't it? He's the all-powerful laying it out for us. Watching us like we're some toys for his fucking amusement. Does he see this coming? Have I outwitted the All-Knowing? Or is this part of the drama he wrote for us?"

Bobby and Jack stare at Danny. Who is this lunatic ranting at us? Their voices start as a whimper and turn into a squall of tears.

A horn sounds sending shock waves through Danny. A light blinds him. He shields his eyes, and through the glare he sees a tugboat, making a straight line for his tiny vessel. God and the Devil may discriminate, but the bow of the oncoming tugboat won't. For all he's worth, Danny beats like a galley slave with one good oar and one short broken oar. The effect is a circular route.

The tug's horn blasts another warning, heard by the ears but felt in the stomach. The boys cry in panic, the boat rocks to extremes, they're not sure whether to hold their ears or hold on to the sides. Deckhands run to the bow of the tugboat, waving their arms and shouting to get out of the way. A searchlight rains down on the rowboat.

Danny's heart pumps like a steam engine ready to blow its gaskets. His arms ache as he pulls against the water. Another blast of the horn, and the rowboat surfs away from the tug's bow. The name *Miss Fortune* steams past. The tug is incapable of stopping even if the captain willed it. A colossal rogue wake runs counter to the wave Danny navigates. It's a clash of powerful forces. Tons of harbor water explode into a mountain, then collapse into a valley. It's over in an instant. The rowboat is swamped and nearly capsizes.

"Bobby," screams Jack.

Danny watches the boy fly across the boat and tumble headlong into the water. The after-wakes separate the boat from the airborne boy. Smacked by an angelic backhand, Danny dives in and swims for Bobby. The kid barely gets a bath, never mind swimming in a commercial shipping lane. Bobby's clothes start to weigh him down. The cold water steals his breath. Just as his head is about to drop below the surface, Danny grabs his hand and pulls him up. A lucky wave rebounds the pair toward the rowboat. The cold water sobers Danny. He focuses on throwing Bobby into the boat. Another wave pushes the boat toward Danny and Bobby.

Danny clutches the boy and holds him above the water. A gentle wave nudges the rowboat. Danny catches the boat before it floats away. He can see it's half full of water. Jack holds on to the seat, paralyzed. There is no way for Danny to get in the boat without tipping it. He can only throw Bobby into the boat and hang on till they bump into shore.

"Come on, lad, in you go." Danny lifts Bobby up, and the boy flops around like a fish refusing to be caught. The boy's foot finds Danny's face and kicks it. It's a knockout punch that sends Danny underwater, taking his breath away.

Danny's lungs are nearly empty. He starts to sink. His nose stings in pain from the mule kick Bobby delivered. The cold water saps his remaining strength. His coat and clothes are dead weight, and his shoes are worse than useless. He looks up and sees nothing but darkness. Around him is a black void, cold and unforgiving. He's sinking at a faster rate. His ears hurt from the water pressure. He can feel his lungs compressing. The urge to breathe is overwhelming.

Danny fights to free himself of his coat, its extra weight pulling him down toward the muck at the bottom. He tears the buttons open and tried to shed this outer skin. His flailing is half successful. He wrestles the coat like a shadow boxer battling demons in the dark. The cuffs are hung up on his wrists. Danny tries to swim upward, but the coat is a sea anchor. Another struggle takes the last bit of air from his lungs. Luck or terror, he manages to rip the cuffs free. His lungs burn. His brain is in revolt between primal need and rational thought. Whichever side wins, the result may be the same.

The shoes, another thought. Get them off and swim, lad. The rational side rages. The primal side agrees and yells—Go for it. Danny curses the laces on his worn-out boots. The idea they would be worthless at a church giveaway and may cost him his life strikes him as poetic. Horrible time for inspiration. Danny fumbles in the dark. Luck, terror, and a knife from his pants pocket slice the laces. Danny, free of his coat, free of his shoes, raises his arms toward the surface. He kicks and waves his arms and begins to ascend.

Danny drifts into the space between life and death. The pain in his ears is gone, and his lungs no longer want. Orbs of light streak through the darkness like shooting stars. Thousands of mortal souls collide in the abyss. They all seem close enough to touch, yet they remain distant and unattainable. The arc of his life reveals itself: births, deaths, good times and bad, friends for life and friends he let go, each its own self-illuminating sphere. Rites of passage, baptism, communion, confirmation, surround him in a loving glow. Danny spins in his ascent, trying to touch the images, to make them real. As they came, they disappear, leaving Danny alone in the dark.

The low drone of diesel engines spin their propellers like a celestial choir filling the emptiness. Out of the void, blooming like a flower, comes an angel. Dressed in a gown of pure white, flowing with the current, she walks on a sea of stars. Her long dark hair floats like a halo, and she wears a white veil on one side of her face. She extends a soldier's belt and presents it as a gift. Danny reaches for it, but she drops it into the dark. The angel blows him a kiss and fades away.

The primal side renews its war against the rational. The lack of air makes thinking impossible. The urge to breathe pries Danny's jaws open. He vomits in reflex, the need for air has taken over. Danny looks up and sees a shining round light, like a shimmering communion wafer, calling him. His mouth opens, and water comes rushing in, filling his empty lungs. He submits. The last thing he sees is St. Peter's hand reaching down through the light, trying to reach him.

It's a guy in a skiff and a searchlight from a passing barge. An old weathered waterman rips Danny out of the harbor and onto the boat. Another waterman, younger, helps pull Danny from the drink.

"Grab him. That's it. Nice and easy." They stretch Danny out and pump his chest to get the water out. The old man has to ask. "What kind of an idiot takes his kids out fishing at a time like this?"

Danny's eyes open and he sees the weathered old man looking down at him. Then he's caught in a round of violent puking.

"That's it, boy. Let it out." The old waterman has dealt with a few soggy men before.

"Kids?" Danny asks. His eyes are large with hope.

"We got them before the rowboat went down. Eddie, get the boys," the old man orders.

Danny sits up as Jack and Bobby jump on him. He holds them tight and kisses their wet little heads. Reason takes hold of him. If it didn't show him a clear path, he clearly knew which path not to follow.

"Your kids, eh?" the old man asks.

Danny looks up, wipes his nose and eyes with his sleeve, and answers, "You bet, sir. You bet they are."

He holds the boys out at arm's length and looks them over. He doesn't see the Devil's kin. He sees only Helen's children.

Danny checks out their situation. The boys are freezing and soaked in their holiday sailor suits. Danny himself is freezing and soaked, without shoes, coat, or money. He has to laugh. There is no place else for his emotions to go. He's alive, Jack is alive, and fucking Bobby is alive. Maybe God made two angels out of the Devil. Wouldn't that be the ultimate joke?

"Ahh shite. Your mother is not going to like this." Danny shakes his head and pulls the boys close.

24: October 21, 1919: Tom Willis's grandmother's house

"How long he gonna be here?" a little kid asks his grandmother.

"As long as he needs, child." An elderly woman strokes the child's hair. "Now go fetch me some blankets and some wet towels. We got to sweat the devil out of him."

Tom expresses concern. "We got to get his ass out of here before Moses gets back."

"Watch your tongue child, you're not so big I won't put a switch to you. I'll take care of Moses. Right now we got to get Mr. Danny well and on his feet." The elderly woman wipes Danny's forehead.

Danny has been asleep for at least fourteen hours. Fourteen rough hours of sweating, vomiting, shitting, and screaming. He wanders in and out of consciousness, only to fall back into a dreamy fit. He doesn't know yet that Tom Willis found Danny and the boys lost and shivering on the docks before dawn. Lucky for Danny, there weren't any trucks for Tom. Tom brought them to his grandmother's house. Some of at the Willis family got the boys bathed and fed. They got Danny into a bed with plenty of blankets to sweat through.

Danny floats in and out of reality. He mumbles unlinked names and words as if he's reciting an incoherent poem. Tom hears a pattern and realizes it's Danny's address. It's time to take the boys home. The trip isn't very far—a simple matter of walking a few extra blocks. Except the matter wasn't simple. On Tom's side of the street, everyone wants to know what he's doing with two little white sailor boys. On the other side of the street, everyone wants to know what trouble is brewing with these little sailor boys and the Colored. Tom feels the stares but knows he's on a mission the Lord handed him. It's not supposed to be easy. Straight ahead, Tom carries Jack and Bobby on his back because they have no shoes.

Grandma Willis's house is a harbor for generations of Willises. There are cousins, aunts, and uncles tossed in; the place is crowded. Moses is the patriarch. He is away working as a conductor on the B&O Railroad. As far as he's concerned, the house is full of unwanted relatives. He won't be happy about a freeloading white boy in his house.

There's a rhythm of people coming and going here. Someone is always going to work, and someone is always returning. Doesn't matter if it's day or night. The kitchen is a twenty-four hour restaurant which Grandma Willis runs with authority. It's possible she may not have slept since 1906. If the young ones get to school, then the house can be quiet for an hour during the day. Maybe that's when she takes a nap.

Danny is going through delirium tremens on a cot in the dining room. The little ones sit around him for amusement. There's a cross hanging on the wall. A sculpted wooden Christ looks down at Danny in pity. Grandma Willis wipes Danny down and helps him drink some water. It doesn't go down well and doesn't stay there.

"Oh Christ, save me." Danny throws up into a bucket.

"He's the only one who can, honey." Grandma Willis pats Danny on the back. "That's the Devil coming out. We got to get some Jesus in you when you're able."

Tom puts his hand on his grandmother's shoulder. She pats his hand and rests her chin on his arm. Her boy was raised right.

"This is the burden we bear as Christians. Even in the heart of the dumbest white boy lives Jesus. It's our burden to roll that stone off his heart and free Jesus. Right now a lot of ugly is going to come out of him. We need buckets, rags, and fresh sheets. Tomorrow he'll be ready to drink some water, or he'll be dead. Either way, he'll be in the Lord's hands."

Tonight Danny discovers a level of pain he thought impossible. As horrific as events in Ireland were—and drowning in the harbor as near to death as God allowed—none compares to this night. They call it the "horrors"— how eloquently understated. If given a choice, he'd choose the bullet over this agony. A cruel angel or playful devil keep Danny alive.

Throughout the night, Danny caroms between delirium and lucid needs. His past demons escape through white-hot flashes of memory. Suddenly he's thirsty. Yet the smell of fresh water and a drop on his lips send him to nausea. His stomach argues for food, yet the idea of a breadcrumb makes his bowels spin like a cement mixer.

Grandma Willis keeps vigil over Danny's delirium. Prayers and wet rags keep him breathing. The old woman knows every gospel hymn ever written and will sing them all until Jesus brings Danny home or keeps him here on earth.

While the call for the rapture may be playing out in the dining room, the rest of the household begs to sleep. The young ones bury their heads under the pillows while the aunts and uncles pray for the lad's quick and lasting recovery. Anything to get Danny out of the house. It's a coin toss which is worse, Danny's delirious cries or Grandma Willis's gospel singing.

The next day, Danny's eyes wake to a headache beyond all hangovers. He's starving and needs something to drink. Anything. Even water or milk. The room around him is unfamiliar. The cot he lies in is soaked from his own sweat. The shades are pulled down, keeping the sun out, but it's still too bright. His feet hit the ground. He's as unsteady as a newborn calf.

"Go back to bed. I'll get you some clean clothes and something to eat. You've been asleep, at least in bed for awhile." Grandma Willis comes into the room.

"Where am I? Where's Bobby and Jack?"

"Don't you worry. My son Tom found you and brought you home like a stray cat. Then he took the little ones to their house. I think you are going to have some fast talking to do when you get home."

"Oh, Christ." Danny drops his head and rubs his hands through his greasy hair.

"Watch your tongue in this house. I don't put up with taking the Lord's name in vain."

"I'm sorry. That might have been a prayer. I don't know." Danny is going to need a lot of help to explain this to Helen. "Can I ask your name?"

"You just call me Grandma like everyone else. I don't know if I answer to my child name anymore."

"What was that?"

"Delia."

"No." Danny smiles in pleasant disbelief. "That's me grand-mammy's name."

Grandma Willis wipes Danny's face. The angel inside Danny is starting to show. His blue-grey eyes are brightening. His voice sounds a little stronger.

"There is some tea on the stove and crackers in the cupboard if you're ready?" Grandma Willis has her hand on Danny's chest as if he's a member of the family on the mend.

"That would be grand, m'am. Where's Tom?"

"He read the newspaper and said he saw an opportunity, so he was out the door." Grandma Willis gets up and heads toward the kitchen. "Here, I don't know what he read, but if your eyes can focus, here's the newspaper."

Danny takes the paper in hand and is stunned. He stares at the front page with his mouth wide open.

"Oh, dear. I didn't mean to embarrass you. You do know how to read?" Grandma Willis puts her hand over her heart.

The headline screams off the page. The photo underneath tells the grisly story.

25: October 21, 1919, 4:00 pm: Baltimore

Helen sits on a battered, overstuffed chair, her knees bent up under her chin. Her tea cooled off a while ago and the crackers sit beside the cup untouched. Outside, the world moves as if nothing had happened. The clouds and the sun can't decide which way the rest of the day will go.

Last night was a disaster. There was the idiot boy, who just pissed her off, and then there was....

Why did that man do that? Why couldn't he just wait his turn? Where does this leave me? Helen thinks about her queendom left unprotected. She can't leave that place for too long. The rats will infest it soon enough.

Helen keeps her eyes on the street, waiting for the knock on the door, expecting the police at any minute. It's quiet here, safe like a womb. She thinks for a moment about the silence. Something isn't right. It's never quiet in the apartment. Usually the twins are screaming or breaking something. Then there's Danny. Even if they don't talk to each other, he is always making noise. If he isn't burping, he's farting; if neither of them, he's puking from a hangover. When he's passed out, sleeping is worse. He snores like a lumber mill. Danny can be unconscious for twelve hours at time. At worst it's a splinter in the ear that can't be dug out. Now the place is as silent as a tomb. Something is wrong, but Helen can't take that in.

Her clothes from last night sit soaking in a bucket. The water has turned blood red. Helen, barely twenty, has as many notches on her belt as an IRB assassin. What kind of life is this? How many men has she fucked and still never been properly kissed? What would it take to start again from birth?

"Would you like some more tea, dear?" Margie asks.

"What?" Helen's mind is far away, but returns at a methodical pace.

"Tea? Would you like some more? Oh, I see you still haven't drunk it yet." Margie takes a look out of the window and pretends to be interested in the weather. "Looks like the sky can't make up its mind. I think a storm is on the way."

Helen turns away in her chair. She just wants to sit here and suck her thumb in a fetal position.

Margie gets a frustrated look on her face.

"All right. Let it out. What happened?" Margie stands over Helen like an irate parent. "You're more beat up than usual. Look at those marks on you. How are you going to explain those to Danny? And where the hell is himself and the boys? Have you given them a thought? Hiding under the covers. What did you do? Kill someone?"

Helen looks up with a blank look. She hadn't given anyone a thought.

"I don't know how much of this nonsense I can take from you and Danny. There's secrets and trouble every time I turn around." Margie turns her back and taps her foot. "Do you even know where they are? Danny and the boys have been gone since yesterday."

Helen jumps out of the chair. That explains the silence. She looks around the small apartment as if Margie overlooked something.

There's a knock at the door. Aunt Margie waves Helen off and goes to answer it. Helen gets nervous. Maybe it's the police.

"It better be Danny and the boys. Who is it?" Margie asks while opening the door. She's stunned and stands with her mouth wide open when she sees who it is. "Oh shit." She slams the door.

Margie puts her back to the door like she's keeping an invading horde at bay. Terror washes over her. She flushes in panic.

"There's a n… nig… at the door. I think he's here to kill Frank."

"Frank's not here," Helen states.

"Christ! I know. He is in debt to his eyes. He's hiding somewhere. Horses, cards, dice, the man is a loser. He couldn't win even if you spot him a three quarter mile lead." Margie's heart races like the horses that cause so much trouble. "Maybe that nig… n… going to kill us instead."

There is another knock on the door. Helen pushes Margie aside with her hurling stick in hand. Nobody is coming in here without a fight.

"Frank's not here!" Helen yells through the door.

She opens the door and finds a Colored as big as a mountain. She looks up at him and sees a smile in return.

"Evening m'am. My name is Tom. Are these yours?" The colored man named Tom steps aside, revealing two little boys in their best sailor suits. The hurling stick falls to the floor.

Helen can't say anything. Her mouth just flops around with nothing coming out.

Bobby and Jack stand in front of their mother, happy as can be. Their little sailor suits have been cleaned and ironed. The pleats in their shorts are sharp enough to slice beef. Both boys have their hair brushed and nicely parted to one side. They are both clean. No dirt smudges on the knees and elbows. No grime under their noses. For a moment Helen wonders if they are, in fact, her kids.

"We went for a boat ride, Mommy," Jack blurts out.

Helen grapples with what's in front of her—her boys, a Colored, and no Danny. Christ—now what?

"Where are their shoes?" Helen looks at the boys' feet. The boys show off their toes like little trophies.

"Don't know nothing about the shoes, m'am." Tom can only smile. Mainly because that's what he always does around white ladies. Smile.

"Where the fuck is Danny?"

"He's with my grandma," Tom answers. "He's sick. She'll fix him or he belongs to Jesus."

The Arrest

1: October 23, 1919, 6:00 am: Great American Meat Company

Mr. Schlamp is at his desk, looking as if he has already been there for hours. He goes through a mountain of papers and finds the one he is looking for. He pulls his pocket-watch out and checks the time. The second hand sweeps past the minute hand. For a second, all the watch hands are facing straight up or down. It is precisely six in the morning. Mr. Schlamp looks up from his watch, and the door knocks on time.

"Come in." Schlamp sits back in his chair to greet his morning business.

Two men walk in. They couldn't be more different. The first to enter is the diminutive foreman, full of his normal morning rage. Behind him walks in a magnificent example of the kind of laborer needed at a slaughterhouse. A very large man, thick arms and neck, legs like a draft horse; best, he is very quiet. He's a Colored.

"This is your new man." Schlamp points to the man with a wry grin. "Willis. Thomas Willis. Willis, this is the foreman. He's your boss."

Willis tips his cap.

"What? Is this a joke?" The foreman spins between the new man and his boss. He leans in toward Mr. Schlamp. "You know he's a nigger."

The foreman looks over his shoulder to see Willis standing without expression. Schlamp looks down at some paperwork, then up at his foreman.

"There is nothing about his being a Colored in the paperwork. It does say he fought in the war. Army, worked as a mechanic—biplanes. Maybe after he gets used to the place you can find something that fits his skills. The American Meat Company likes to hire our fighting men when possible." Schlamp holds a hand to his ear. "Did you fight in the war?"

"No." The foreman is frustrated by the only answer he can give. "But still. A nigger? The boys on the floor aren't going to like this."

"They don't have to. Any man who will work cheap is welcome here, no matter if he's colored, chink, dago, mick. The war is over. Things are changing. You and the boys better be ready. Pretty soon I'll have a sober second shift. Maybe not so many fingers in the ground beef, eh?"

2: October 23, 1919, 9:00 am: Henry Weiss's funeral

The sky is a deep gray. Nature's colors have drained away to black and white. It gives the church steeple a menacing look. A cold autumn wind stirs up the dead leaves in little tornadoes outside St. Mary's. Men in black suits stand on the church steps smoking cigarettes and passing a thermos of coffee around.

Inside the church, in the front row, sitting alone, is Mrs. Weiss. She's dressed in black, veiled in mourning. Her eyes are bloodshot, and her nose is a red sore. There's no organ music. The only sound is the footsteps of an old man on the marble floor. Hunched over, cane in hand, dressed in army green, a member of the Veterans Society, he comes up and gives Mrs. Weiss a flag and a handshake. He walks over to the coffin and salutes. With the speed of a sundial's shadow, he turns around and exits through the back of the church.

Incense fills the sanctuary. Bells ring. Smoke rises to the dome. A celestial scene, painted years ago, waits for Henry's soul to ascend. The dome is filled with cherubs blaring trumpets and beating drums, celebrating a crucified Christ among the clouds. Once the pride of the parish, today the ceiling's leaky roof creates yellow stains. The chipping plaster threatens the congregation.

Father O'Donnell proves his faith every service under the threatening dome, hands raised. The service begins. He speaks God's language, Latin. His words reverberate off the stone walls, droning on with celestial authority. Mrs. Weiss cries.

Father O'Donnell approaches the pulpit to give Henry's eulogy.

"Henry Weiss." The name rebounds throughout the church. The priest looks around the sanctuary. The plaster statues stand coldly uninterested. There is a hardness all around. Torturous wooden pews, fieldstone walls, stone icons, stained-glass windows, marble floors, how much more like a tomb than a place of celebration. It's not a sanctuary of the soul; it's a gothic fortress. Votive prayer candles illuminate hopes and prayers, yet not one for Henry. The empty pews tell the story of Henry Weiss.

The pastor clears his throat. Anything he has to say about Henry would only be a trite recap of a hundred other funerals he's served. Father O'Donnell didn't really know Henry, just the shame put on him as a young boy. After that, Henry was lost. The priest sees himself partly responsible for a young man's death. No, he didn't pull the weapon that snuffed Henry's life, any more than he was the priest that sinned. Yet O'Donnell sees himself as a link in a horrible chain. Looking down at the mother, he has nothing to say. In fact, the whole service has the stink of bullshit. The priest steps down from the pulpit. He kneels before the sacrament and turns toward an altar boy. Carefully the priest removes his stole, gives it a kiss, and hands it to the mystified altar boy. He unties the cincture around his waist and again hands it off. Slowly he removes his chasuble, the outer vestment priests wear. Stripped down to his white tunic, Father O'Donnell kneels, and then comes off the altar.

"Louise." Father O'Donnell holds his hands out. "Louise, let's go bury your son."

Six men in dark suits enter the church quietly; with professional efficiency, they remove the casket. Father O'Donnell puts his arm around Louise Weiss and helps the old woman follow her son down the center aisle. He thinks, this is the opposite of a wedding—when the parents lead the children to the altar to the lifelong union. Today Henry leads his mother from the altar to his bride, the earth. It's a union that will not be broken until the Resurrection. Maybe this is the peace that Henry never found in life. Did the angels and demons play games of chance for his soul? How different could it have been, had he just gone to a different church? What if he had just gone home that gruesome night, instead of running with hoodlums? Father O'Donnell grins, mocking himself. He is supposed to have these answers. How is he supposed to speak of Henry's life? He decides this is the most priestly thing he could do—shed his priestly garments.

Louise Weiss doesn't see them. The Latin is sad-sounding mumbo-jumbo. It's time for compassion, not mandated ceremony. Father O'Donnell holds Louise Weiss close and shuts up.

3: October 23, 1919, 3:00 pm: Baltimore Public School 23

Napoleon leans against a streetlamp, head down. His wool cap hides his face. The collar on his duster is up, keeping the chill off his neck. He puffs a cigarette impatiently. Inside the school, across the street, his crew is held captive till the bell rings.

The school clock strikes three. The bell rings and the doors fly open. Screams and yells drown out the street traffic. The headmistress stands at the top of the steps, a conductor overseeing a chaotic orchestra. Napoleon throws his cigarette butt to the ground and walks silently toward the school. He strides defiantly toward the headmistress to make his presence known. She looks like anyone's grandmother. Plump, with white hair in a strict bun, her clothes every kind of gray. Whatever sweetness she has vanishes at the sight of Napoleon.

Napoleon stands in front of the mistress. With a snap of his fingers, he reveals his fangs. Little Olie works his way through the stream of schoolchildren to give Napoleon a cigarette. His crew assembles around him at the bottom of the steps. Whitey steps up with a match, and Napoleon breathes life into his cigarette. The headmistress looks at the boys, wondering what attracted them to this hoodlum.

Napoleon takes a drag off his cigarette and blows the smoke toward the school. He tips his cap to the headmistress, as polite as any gentleman, and leads his crew into the late afternoon.

4: October 23, 1919, 5:45 pm: Majewski gets ready

A threatening sky keeps its promise and unleashes its fury. There's a low rumbling that builds to a crescendo, then explodes in a boom rattling the windows. Detective Majewski looks out the window near his desk. Day turns to night in a moment. Another low rumbling, then another boom. Majewski clutches the arm of his desk chair. A third blast of thunder puts him into a cold sweat. A torrent of rain lashes against the windows.

Majewski rubs his temples. The thunder sets off a train of thought he prefers not to board. His hips hurt. Panic is creeping in. His doctor gave him some medicine to take in these situations. In his desk lies the escape from pain. A finely crafted leather pouch is tucked under some papers. Inside is a small vial of white powder and a spoon that looks as if it came from a doll's tea set. Majewski opens it up carefully, dips the spoon, and gathers as much as it will allow. He brings the spoon to his nose, gently, so not to spill a grain. He holds his other nostril closed so nothing sneezes out. It's gone in a snort. He repeats the process for the other nostril. Carefully, he returns the vial to his desk and leans back in his chair. Outside, the thunder becomes more frequent and flashes of lightning light up his small office. Majewski closes his eyes and submits to the thunder and lightning. It reminds him of his recent past.

Majewski had become a mounted officer in the cavalry of romance. He had seen himself a mounted warrior, leading the charge with a drawn sword, flags flying, with the courage of sunrise.

That warrior held doubts. His wife left him for a fancy cook she'd met somehow, and she took his son with her. The hole left behind needed to be filled. He left the police force, joined up, and waited for America to enter the war. From peace to war, from a dead stop to full throttle, the country did join the war, and Majewski went with it.

Romance shed its skin quickly. Instead of creating gallant warriors, the mounted corps was reduced to messengers, scouts, or machine gun food. They say "time heals all wounds." Well, enough time hasn't passed. Four hundred and ninety-nine days isn't enough. Majewski has the date imprinted on his brain: June 11, 1918, Belleau Wood, north of Paris.

The Germans were brutal. Their machine-gun fire cut down waves of Marines like harvesting summer wheat. Majewski and his horse were part of the communications link between the 6th Machine Gun Battalion, 2nd Battalion, and 2nd Engineers. He shuttled between commands regularly, but his routes were hard to follow. Around him, the landmarks changed constantly. Church steeples disappeared; houses, barns, whole village blocks—all vanished and rendered to rubble. The air was filled with smoke and gunpowder, then the worst, wafts of mustard gas, drifted from the German line. On June 11th, Majewski became disoriented in the amber haze and was lost behind the enemy line.

Belleau Wood was on fire. The Devil used French and American artillery like apocalyptic billiard balls indiscriminately bashing into everything. Trees became blackened skeletons reaching heavenward, creating a surreal landscape. North, south, left, right; directions made no difference under a rain of artillery. Thunder and explosions surrounded Majewski, throttling his gut. He realized he was caught in storm of friendly artillery, a term the Germans would not have used. *Maybe Henry Weiss loaded one of these shells.* That would be a sad irony. Somewhere in the haze, he heard voices pleading in French. Majewski and his horse moved through a nightmare toward the voices. As he got closer, the cries became louder, and the form of several people on their knees took shape.

At first Majewski could hear nothing but the clip-clop of his horse's hooves. Then the image of civilians, hands raised in surrender, became clear. He looked around to see who they were surrendering to. His mount's trot began to speed up. Two German soldiers appeared out of the mist. Fulfilling his romantic warrior's need, Majewski drew his sword and charged. A khaki-clad knight kicked his steed hard. The nature of time changed. He felt as if he were underwater, fathoms deep, breathing hard, driving his horse to rescue the innocent. The German gun barrels become bigger. He could see the soldiers' fingers on the triggers. Shells exploded, and chunks of earth rained on him. The cry of "Mercy!" intensified. Majewski screamed "Halt!" to no effect. "*Mercy—Bitte!*" No amount of pleading was able to stop the Germans from taking aim. Majewski felt helpless to stop the execution. He threw his sword at the soldiers. It landed harmlessly. Strapped to his back was his Enfield rifle. From gallop to top speed, his horse bolted through battle's haze. Majewski took aim. There was an earsplitting whistle, an explosion, a blinding light, then nothing. When Majewski could see again, he was alive in a nightmare. He saw his mount dismembered and caught in barbed wire. Around him was nothing—nothing. There was a crater where there had been something. Now there were no humans to be found.

A knock on the office door snaps Majewski from his thoughts.

"Who is it?" Majewski straightens his tie and wipes his eye.

"It's the men, sir. I have them lined up for briefing."

"I will be there presently." Majewski adjusts his shoulder gun holster and positions his badge just right on his lapel.

5: October 23, 1919, 11:45 pm: The Arrest

A shroud of fog covers the harbor. Ship horns moan like ghosts. The air is saturated, bulging with of rain. Gas-lamps line the streets in a ghostly glow. It's the kind of night where honest people stay home.

Detective Majewski is given four uniformed patrolmen to make his arrest. After tonight, the case will remain open but not active. There are always new cases and ever more important people who need justice. The plan is simple. A few blocks away, the paddy wagon, with two additional men, waits for a whistle. Foot patrolmen will take positions around the statue, behind the bushes, spring-loaded. The men tell the old joke, you can tell which way is north because General Lee's ass points that way. It's a handy way to get your bearings.

"Gentlemen, the weather is going to make communicating difficult. Be careful, stay quiet. Have your lanterns ready, but keep them off until I give the signal. We are looking for a woman with a scar on her face. Wait for me to make the identification. Be warned, she will be armed with something. She is dangerous." Majewski looks his men over. Two are war vets like himself, and two are new to the force and seem anxious. "Also, this could be more than a woman acting alone. The victim was a big man and had an ice pick in his throat. She may very well have an accomplice, or it's a gang. Let's wait until she attracts some business and sees what happens before we move in."

"Sir, one question." A senior patrolman steps forward.

"What is it?"

"How do we know if she will come back here tonight, or ever again? I mean she did do someone in right here. I figure she figures the spot too hot or unlucky." The patrolman rubs his chin.

"Good question. It is a bit of a crapshoot, I admit. But I get the feeling she is territorial. Even if the weather isn't great, I'll bet she will be out here just to defend her turf if nothing else." Majewski looks for more questions.

The policemen follow Majewski into the park. The foul weather hasn't done much to curb a deviant's appetite. Majewski's flesh crawls as he walks through a menagerie of fetishes. Each dark corner offers the releases various perverts require.. All one has to do is pay. The sight of the uniforms sends the human vermin scampering off like cockroaches caught in a gaslight. This doesn't sit well with Velvet—or Alice, as her mother calls her.

"What the hell, Majewski?" Alice walks up to the detective, arms akimbo.

"Shh." Majewski puts his finger to his lips. "We are looking for the one with the scar."

"I told you, she works the statue. Don't make our lives hard."

"Don't worry. I want to make sure she doesn't have any help hiding in the bushes." Majewski places his hand on her shoulder.

"That one doesn't have any help. Trust me." Alice puts her hands on Majewski's collar and pretends to adjust it. "Well, good riddance. You know if you just want to have fun, you can always buy me a drink."

Majewski gets warm inside his overcoat.

Helen unknowingly cooperates and is in her place under General Lee. Her lantern gives everything a supernatural light in the fog. She braces against the statue's base and takes a ritual moment to get herself through the night's labor. How much longer can she endure this way of life? It's not just the endless supply of strange men; it's the dual life she leads. Her husband and boys have been protected from knowing what she does. The boys are too young to understand, and her husband is a drunk who gets dumber by the ounce.

Footsteps echo in the fog. Helen tries to cut through the haze to see where they're coming from. Her eyes are wide, on alert. The steps continue to move slowly, circling her like a predator.

Detective Majewski hears the footsteps as well. He keeps his men under control, like dogs pulling on a leash. If he's lucky, he can catch the prostitute with a customer, then add the charge of murder once she's in custody.

The disembodied footsteps continue to pace around the statue, like ghosts lurking on the edge of the otherworld. Majewski waxes philosophical. The fog enjoys hiding the truth. Wisps of truth float away and rematerializes as something different.

He thinks about Henry Weiss. Found dead here only a few days ago. At first, it seemed a simple robbery gone ugly. The evidence, what little there is, seems obvious. A penniless drunk, pants around his ankles, an ice pick in his throat. But there is another piece of evidence that makes him wonder who the real victim is. There is a barber's clean blade with Weiss's fingerprints on the handle. Not the kind of innocent grooming article a regular fellow carries in his pocket. Then Majewski thinks about the cats. Weiss may be a victim in the grand scheme of life, but he may not be in this small case. The closer he looks at Weiss, the more he needs to know the truth.

The footsteps stop. Her curiosity gets the better of her. The steps start again and move behind her. Defensively, she turns on her heels, like a sentry on duty. Helen walks toward the sound. A few hard nights and a few bruises were the results when she couldn't control the situation. That's why she has rules. Tonight the fog compromises the security of her queendom. An invader is taking his time. Perhaps this is how he gets his fun? A playful pervert who enjoys terrifying simple women of the night? Does she play the femme fatale? Is she the queen of her domain, demanding compliance?

The footsteps get closer; the shape of a man slowly appears. Helen can't make out features, but the man's stance looks familiar. He starts whistling an old Irish tune. His whistling has a melancholy sound to it. It's anything but the joyous birdcall song some tunes have. The fog adds a considerable amount of theatre to this john. It keeps him in silhouette. He dances in half time to his melody. Fantasy or familiarity, there is something about the shadow figure. She blows that idea out of her mind. She's open for business, no time.

"I have two rules. One, no talking, and two, I don't want to see you. If you understand, ring the bell twice." Helen points to the bell on the park bench and takes refuge under the statue.

The figure moves in a circle around the bench. His footsteps sound hollow in the fog. The bell rings twice. Majewski's men twitch in their positions. It's cold and damp, a quick arrest and they all can get some hot coffee and grind out their shift. Majewski holds them in place, waiting for the right moment. For that, the shadow figure needs to buy sex. Majewski has his men stay behind the shrubbery while he circles behind the statue to hear the prostitute's conversation. He moves slow and silent along the paving stones.

The figure picks up the dinner bell. Helen retreats to the statue's base to reveal her wares.

"If you like what you see, ring twice. Once if you don't. It's a raw night, so don't think about it too long." Helen gives that speech a dozen times a night.

Numb to the cold, Helen drops her coat to the ground and shows the merchandise. The bell rings twice.

"That's was easy, come on then, let's get it over with." Helen leans against the statue and offers her bottom with professional nonchalance.

The shadow figure walks into the lamplight. "Helen."

"I said no talking." Helen is pissed her rule has been violated. "How do you know…"

Helen turns to see who calls her by name.

"Oh dear God." Helen feels sick to her stomach as her knees buckle. "Danny? It's you. I thought you left. Where have you been?"

"Aye, 'tis me."

Helen slumps to the paving stones, tears welling in her eyes. She never thought he knew.

"I'm a drunk, not a fool. And I read. I read the newspaper. I can only imagine what you've been through," Danny says.

Helen gets to her knees. Danny lifts her head and sees the bruises under her jaw and around her neck. Pushing back the veil, he looks her in the eyes for the first time in years. "I've got something I have to tell you. I should have said it a long time ago. If only I had. Then maybe we wouldn't be here now."

Through her tears, Helen shakes her head, not knowing what he means.

"I couldn't protect you that day. And now, I still haven't protected you. This is my fault, I couldn't free myself from that tree. That fucking belt has been around my throat for three years. But it happened to you, not me. I would have traded my life for you. Then I just couldn't look those boys in the eyes. Instead, I drank myself into another world to blot out the pain. Your pain, my pain." Danny starts to stammer, tears falling down his cheeks. "I never loved anyone like I love you. I want to hold that girl from Donegal. I want to hold all her innocence. I want to kiss that girl. But I can't, and never will. That day is gone."

Danny fumbles around in his pockets looking for something.

"Here, I wrote this for you." Danny finds a scrap of paper in his pocket and hands it to her.

The paper is crumpled; the words look as if they were written by a shaking hand. Helen wipes her eyes to read the lines. Her mouth moves as her eyes focus on the words. Her head swings back and forth. She frowns.

"Danny, this is dreadful. I mean it's a riddle, not a poem." Helen stands up, pondering. "What does this mean? *Shoes worthless at a church fair, made value of a life.*"

"Never mind. I'll tell you one day. Agh, I know. It's awful. But I wrote it. That's what's important. The next one will be better." Danny starts to smile.

"Jesus, it would have to be. It couldn't be worse." Helen laughs, wiping tears from her face.

"Read the last line." Danny points down at the paper.

Helen mumbles the words. *To these I render apology.*

Fair weather passes, and storm clouds brew in Helen's brain. Somewhere the angels and demons are making bets.

"So you think some odd verse and 'I'm sorry' is going to change anything or pay the bills?" Helen simmers, trying to keep her emotions in check.

"I don't think that. I know it won't be easy." Danny moves toward her.

"You think a few cheap words on paper mean anything? Follow your dreams, you selfish bastard, but I have kids to feed—bills to pay. I don't get to have dreams. Do you have any idea what I go through so you can lay about drunk?" Helen's emotions are boiling over.

Danny has a good idea but is too terrified to say anything.

"Suffering artist—sweet suffering Jesus, what the hell happened to the boys? They leave with you, and they come home with a colored and no shoes. No shoes? Where were you?"

Danny stands frozen. How does he answer that? *Funny thing, I went to drown the kids but lost their shoes.* He's smart enough to know his wife doesn't take guff from anyone and knows she is dangerous, so he keeps his mouth in check.

"I have so much to say I'm sorry about." He doesn't want to think about how she has been spending her nights to provide for him.

"That's not putting shoes on the boys." Helen crumples the poem in her hands and tosses it. "Do you have any idea what I did to get those fucking sailor suits? And you ruin them!"

Helen is in full rage. She hurls two fists at Danny like she's pounding on a door.

"You want to hear what I do to strange men? You want to know how they touch me—for money—so I can buy clothes for my boys?"

"I know. I saw you." Danny can barely get the words out. He picks up the poem and tucks it into his pocket.

Helen is speechless. The fog holds time in place.

"I'm trying to clean up. I'm wearing Uncle Frank's suit. He's nowhere to be found, so I figure it's swell to use it. I know being sober for two days isn't much. But it's a start. I shake like a son of a bitch, but I'm writing. Words, pen to paper. It's like riding a bike, I keep falling off. But I'll get better."

"You mean like falling off a barstool."

"I need you. My heart has no choice but to love you. And that means all of you and your kin. Jack and Bobby. I couldn't accept that, till now. And believe me, I don't want to tell you what it took for me to see the light. We have to stop living in shame." Danny looks at General Lee and wonders who he was that he deserves such a big statue. Helen's coat is on the ground. Danny picks it up and covers Helen's shoulders. "This is no place for a lady."

Danny holds Helen, hoping for something he can't define. He knows the girl from the old days is gone, but in her place is a woman Danny desperately wants to know and love. This new woman has two kids who need him. Something new emerges from the ash of darkness—hope. But Danny is new too.

"Tomorrow the moon and the stars will shine. The angels and devils will play their petty games." Danny holds Helen's hands in his. "We walk on borrowed time, and I need too many borrowed words to reach you."

"All you need to borrow is a fucking guitar. Saints save me from your horrible lyrics." Helen pushes Danny away.

"I know what I say isn't worth its weight in gold. We crossed an ocean and wandered down too many wrong roads to let it all slip away. This all can't be for nothing. I don't expect you to love me like the old days. Hell, we never got a chance. It won't be easy. Give me a chance to find that spark in your heart again. We're better together than apart."

"We've been apart. You just found out."

"I used to work as a newspaperman in the old country. I know the business, from janitor to obituaries. They have newspapers here in Baltimore. If I can't find a job with one of them, it's a big country that doesn't give a shit about Ireland, so I'll find a job somewhere else. Till then there are bars that need tending, floors to be swept, shit to be shoveled." Danny is out of breath, making his case on one leg.

Helen doesn't know whether to beat him or cover him with kisses. Maybe both?

"The bugle calls, and now you wake up. Do you have any idea what I've been through waiting for you to wake up?" Helen shoves him. "Shame? You have no idea what shame is. Every night I live and relive the shame. Every coin I touch is tarnished with shame. Yet we eat."

Danny has no defense. Metaphors mean nothing in a battle of words. Facts are the munition of choice. He's like a nail to a hammer. Head down in surrender, he turns away from his wife.

"No, you don't get it that easy. You don't just get to walk away. You need to know what I do every night to feed my kids and put a roof over your drunken arse." Helen looks at the base of the statue. Her hurley stick sits waiting in the dark. "You live your life between your ears. I have to live in the world with dandies, drunks, degenerates. I have no time for your fucking deep thoughts and apologies."

That stops Danny in his tracks. It wasn't always like this.

"You have a short memory. I put a ring on your finger and saved you from getting butchered or ending up in the convent laundry. That wasn't my job. It wasn't like Prince fucking Charming was going to rescue you." Danny still has some emotional currency. "I made the deal with the Devil to get us out of Ireland."

Helen knows a deal was made for them to get out of Ireland. They told her Danny really didn't have the stomach for rebellion, he'll always be a pawn. She never knew what the plan was in Derry. All she knows is that's where

Danny got the ring. Helen spins the twine around her wedding finger as if she's trying to remember something.

"The Devil has one more play." Helen threatens, moving toward the statue where the hurley axe begs for action.

"Evening, Madam." Out of the mist appears the Baltimore Police Department. Majewski tips his bowler hat toward Helen.

Danny sees the uniformed men and goes into a panic. This isn't going to happen again; he quickly comes to his wife's defense. Danny stands in front of Helen, protecting her from Majewski. As he does the uniforms step closer. The detective holds up his hand, keeping his men back.

"I thought I might ask a few questions, if you don't mind?" Majewski looks Danny over. He had gotten an earful of what the two just said.

"If you don't mind, me and the missus are out for a late walk." Danny makes his stand.

"Do you call that evening walk clothes?" Majewski refers to the tawdry nightgown under Helen's coat.

"The missus has trouble sleeping. So we're out for a walk. We should be getting back. The aunt has the kids," Danny answers.

"I see. Ma'am, you wouldn't know anything about a stabbing, happened here a few nights ago?" Majewski sees a fading bruise around her neck that left fingermarks and black eyes. How did they get there? Looking at Helen's hands, he thinks a fingerprint sample from her would pretty much seal her fate.

Helen takes a deep breath.

Majewski analyses his search for truth and justice. This is just another murder case on the books he needs to resolve. In the grand scheme of things, this crime means little. Another skirmish fought among society's lowest reaches. There is no outrage; flags aren't at half mast. No one is going to miss Henry Weiss. Maybe his mother. She won't last long without him. After that, well, it's not like a gentleman from Bolton Hill is missing. He found Mr. Weiss a troubled man, a flawed man, created by his world. Did Weiss deserve to die cold and alone, drowning in his own blood? He was a working man who helped his mother and served his country. Did he deserve to die at the hands of this woman?

He looks at Helen. He doesn't know anything about her other than the bits and pieces he just heard. Whatever drove her to this life, she has a chance to turn around. There is a man here pleading to take his wife home. Majewski envies Danny's passion. Maybe if he had shown some of that passion to his own wife, she wouldn't be with someone else. Perhaps Majewski might have saved his marriage and be with his boy. Perhaps he would have avoided the Great War and all its glories.

Majewski's job is to prosecute, not judge. It's not for him to decide innocence or guilt. But something bothers him. Fair and equal. They never seem to be the same thing. Sure the law needs to be applied equally, but is it fair? He knows how cruel this world can be, especially in the administration of justice. He looks at his men. Their main concern is to get where it's warm and dry. The strong arm of the law needs a higher standard than that. What happens when this woman goes to court? He doubts she is a citizen. She has no money for any kind of legal defense. A public defender will be eaten alive by a decent prosecutor. Her fingerprints on the ice pick will punch her ticket to hell. By the time she reaches court, her bruises will heal, any proof of an altercation will be gone. Without a good lawyer, a jury of twelve men will have her carted off to the gallows. Is justice served? She leaves behind two kids and a husband, a family destroyed. Would that avenge Henry Weiss? Would that make his mother sleep better at night? Would the future be better served if she goes home with a man who wants to love her and get her off the streets? Would her kids have a better chance in life if their mother is home?

Majewski looks at Helen, searching for a crack in her armor. He prays for a trace of contrition. But he sees too many other unnamed emotions projecting from her eyes. He turns to Danny. He sees a man, heart in hand, hoping for a new start with his wife. She must be quite a lady for him to be willing to make a go of it with a street whore. Majewski looks up to General Lee. The statue looks straight ahead, sword raised, but offers no sage advice.

"Sir, are we going to make an arrest?," one of the uniformed policemen asks.

"Good question, Officer," Majewski replies.

The detective pushes Helen's veil aside and lifts her chin. He sees the fingermarks around her throat, but it's the scar that shapes her face. Helen wears her rough edges like medals of valor. She stands as disciplined as a soldier. She gives nothing away.

"So I'll ask again. Do you know anything about the stabbing here a few nights ago?" Majewski asks.

"Just what was in the newspaper, sir," Helen answers in a monotone.

Majewski doesn't like what he hears. If he at least can have some closure to this case, he can rest his moral struggle. He shakes his head.

"Tell me what I want to hear." With the eye of a seasoned interrogator, Majewski looks into Helen's soul.

The detective's glare grinds Helen down. She never wanted to hurt anyone, but her life was at stake. She'll not take the blame for defending herself, yet there is a lot of blood spilled at her feet. Helen looks away, tears finding their way down her cheeks. The movie newsreel in her mind projects the face of the soldiers that raped her before she shot at them. A crudely spliced montage of the old prostitute who scarred her and that hulking brute who tried to strangle her, prove her to be dangerous on the street. Helen will never be able to let go of their final moments. To take a life is very godlike. But gods don't have mixed emotions. Helen is mortal, and these faces will haunt her forever. Does she feel remorse? That isn't the word.

"I can't." Helen knows the word, and she is not ashamed—victorious. The detective doesn't want to hear that, he wants a poor immigrant girl to feel sorry. Helen looks at him from her emotional fortress. Revenge, that's another dirty word nobody wants to admit. That's the word that fills that hole where dignity is uprooted. By her count, the world has three fewer sinners. Victory is hard won, and instead of medals of valor, she will live with the nightmare and stain of each battle.

"Your lordship, it's getting late. I should take the missus home." Danny plays his 'poor immigrant in need' role to the hilt.

"Sir, are we going to make an arrest?" the uniformed policeman asks again.

Majewski takes a long look at Helen. He has no doubt she placed the ice pick in Henry Weiss's throat. Why? He has to know.

"I'm not sure." Majewski moves slowly around Helen. She locks her stare on the stone general's stirrups.

Majewski stands behind Helen and bends down into her ear. He whispers, "Tell me what I want to hear."

Christ, I want to scream, roars through Helen's mind. Yet she matches the bronze general in outward emotion.

"Helen, let's go." Danny stretches his hand out.

Helen comes out of her trance and looks at her husband. He looks so hopeful. She turns to the detective. He wears hope on his face as well. *Why the hell is so much hope pinned on me?*

"Let's go home." Danny holds Helen around the shoulders and tries to get her moving. The policemen react like chess pieces, checking their exit.

"Tell me what I want to hear," Majewski asks again.

Helen gives Danny a long look, then kisses him on the mouth.

"I'm sorry." Helen's emotions let loose, like a dam breaking. She is speaking only to Danny.

Majewski feels the weight tumble off his shoulders. The truth will come out now. The angels have shown all their cards. What does the Devil win?

Majewski points to his number two. "Cuff her."

Danny moves to protect his wife, but two policemen restrain him. He tries to fight them off, in vain. Majewski blows his whistle and the paddy wagon siren replies. The headlights appear in the fog. Helen has her hands behind her back in handcuffs. Two patrolmen escort her down the paved stone path into the mist.

Danny's resistance is rewarded with a nightstick to the head. Bashed to the ground, he tries to get up.

"Helen. No!"

"Stay down, boy." Another smack with a nightstick and Danny hits the paving stones face-first. His cheeks are shredded by the rough rocks. A foot lands on the back of his neck, forcing his nose into the ground. The smell of dead leaves and dirt reminds Danny of the grave, a shit time for inspiration. He struggles under the foot on his neck, then a knee lands in the middle of his back.

The fog creeps in, the wind starts to swirl. A mist turns to drizzle to a torrent. Wind and rain blind Danny. Blurry shapes struggle into the paddy wagon. He hears Helen screaming, "Get off me, you fucking bastards."

The motor starts up, the siren winds up, and Helen is taken away in the night.

"That's it, then." The two uniforms holding Danny in place release him. "Now be a good lad. Go home. You're better off without the whore."

"She's my wife." Danny strikes one of the policemen off guard with a respectable left hook.

"Fuck off." The two policemen turn around and give Danny a thorough beating. They pummel him to the paving stones. Danny curls up in a fetal position to absorb the punishment. The two uniforms take turns giving Danny swift kicks to the ribs. Just a reminder of who the law is around here.

Above, in the clouds, above the lightning and thunder, the eternal games of chance play on. The angel chalks his cue stick, while the demon breaks a new rack.

The rain runs down General Lee's bronze face like tears.